Mistress Manor

Mistress Manor

M Ross

1

Chapter One

Bridgett had been sold after spending six out of the ten years since her and Marcus had parted ways at the training house for submissives and dominates. Even though Marcus had helped teach her the art of dominance and submission four years after they had gone their separate ways, she had started to crave something that she couldn't seem to find on her own, and instead of seeking Marcus out she had found a house that trained those inclined to learning the art of dominance and submission. So, she had learned and gotten back some of what had been missing.

But now the house had sold her for sixty thousand dollars, and she was to be a submissive to some snotty young buck of a lord. At the moment she was being washed and oiled in preparation for her first night as the lords sub. When the collar was placed around her throat she sighed in resigned acceptance and was led from the bathing chamber to the lord's playroom to wait.

She didn't have to wait long for he was already there and naked with a drink in his hand.

"Awe my new prize has arrived." He said with a leer as he walked towards her.

"Leave us." He barked to the servant who had led her to the room.

"Now my prize it's time to have some fun." He grabbed the leash attached to the collar and pulled her to him for a drunken sloppy kiss.

Breaking the kiss, he pulled her roughly over to a hip high table pushing her onto her back. After he gulped the last of his drink, he began strapping her down. Stretching her arms above her head he cinched her wrists a bit too tight with the leather strap before moving down to open her thighs. When the leather bit into the flesh of her right thigh she winced slightly, and the lord slapped her pussy when he saw.

"No flinching sub, I do what I please to those I own." With that said he strapped her left thigh down just as tight.

Stepping back some the lord took his meaty cock in hand stroking it fast and hard until he blew a thick creamy load onto the pink wet folds of her pussy. When he finished panting, he walked over to a rack of toys, and choosing a ruler sized piece of wood that had metal studs on it he returned to her. Then starting at her collarbone worked his way down her right side striking her flesh every few inches, reaching her open thighs he used both hands to flick the ruler from her knee inward to where her thigh met her hip. Still using both hands he then snapped it against her pussy six times ripping a scream from her lips with each stroke, laughing at this he stepped back again gripping his cock and jerking off till her pussy was once again coated in his cum.

Walking to her left shoulder he began working his way down snapping the ruler against her pussy even harder this time, but instead of stepping back to jerk off he dropped the toy and fucked his thick cock thru her tender flesh pounding her pussy until he came once again in her hot core only to walk away leaving her strapped to the table as he collapsed on the bed into sleep.

Bridgett stared up at the ceiling, what the hell was that? Her body was throbbing from the points the studded ruler had made contact, and her throbbing pussy was dripping his cum mixed with her own wetness, and her unattended desire left to burn inside. She must have drifted off because sometime later she was jerked awake as the lord pulled her off the table by the leash, and forced her onto a spanking bench, the straps biting into her flesh as the lord secured her to it before gripping her hair and forcing his cock deep into her mouth and fucking over and over, and when she gagged and coughed as he came in her mouth he pulled out and slapped her hard enough to split her lip before gagging her and picking up a flogger. The lord worked her back and ass over and over with the flogger, the blows getting harder and harder until he finally dropped the toy only to grip her hair before fucking her fast and hard from behind.

Two hours later when the lord had decided he was done playing with her he led her to a small chamber. Chaining her wrists above her to the bed he left her there and went to find his own bed.

Marcus sat at the back of the tavern with a bottle of whiskey half gone at his elbow scanning the room through a drunken haze. It had been ten years since he had parted ways with Bridgett, and he had spent the better part of those years at the bottom of the bottle. He had taken lovers over the years, but he eventually would see Bridgett in their submission, and he wouldn't be able to stand the sight of them anymore so he would leave without a word. Sneaking off in the dead of night moving to another town.

Now he was contemplating taking on another sub or going to find Bridgett and demand that they work things out finding a way to forge ahead together. But instead of moving or starting to make a plan he lifted his glass continuing to drown himself in booze.

A few hours later and halfway into his second bottle he stared as a petite redhead sashayed her way over to him. Her hips and breasts heavily accented by the black corset that cinched in her narrow waist. When the woman reached his table and leaned in, he gripped her hair pulling her in for a drunken kiss thrusting his tongue deep tasting honey and wine. When the woman moaned in response, he pulled her onto his lap moving his exploration to her throat and the swell of her plump tits while working his free hand under her skirts to stroke her thigh. Rubbing at her inner thigh getting closer and closer to her bare folds when he reached them, he found them soaked with her juices, he groaned against her throat biting down on her pale flesh.

"Oh, sire give me more..." the woman moaned at his bite squeezing his fingers as her thighs clinched in desire.

"More you say." He pulled back staring into her lust clouded eyes.

"Please sire..." she begged so sweetly.

He silently pulled his hands away and forced her to stand as he did. Taking the bottle with one hand while taking the nape of her neck in the other. He walked them to the stairs in the corner and pushed her up ahead of him.

In his penthouse suite above the tavern, he set the bottle aside and silently stripped her of her clothes petting and teasing her heated flesh as it was exposed. When she was fully naked, he cuffed her wrists with his hands behind her and walked her backwards to the bed pushing her onto it with her arms still behind her. Stepping back, he stared as he undid his pants freeing his stiff cock. When he gripped it stroking its length the woman moaned arching her back. Still without a word Marcus stroked the tip of his cock through her wet folds before thrusting into her hot pussy to the hilt.

"Sire..." she said on a low moan of desire.

Seeing the lust and desire in her eyes and her body Marcus fucked her fast and hard listening to her chanted sire over and over. When he finally came feeling her convulse around him, he pulled out with one word.

"Stay." And he walked away retrieving the bottle before heading to the bathroom.

Marcus shut himself in the bathroom leaning his forehead against the cool wood of the door. Did he really want to do this? Did he even know what he was doing? With a deep sigh he took a swig from the bottle still in his hand, and opening the door again went to take care of the sub on his bed.

Returning to the woman on his bed he slowly began stroking the tops of her thighs, bending down he kissed her naval before slipping his arms under her low back to help her into a sitting position. Rubbing her back, he took her lips in a soft drugging kiss, the honey on her lips tasted so good he wanted more and more, but he wanted to play as well so he broke the kiss and helped her to stand. Gripping the back of her neck he gave her another brief kiss before walking her over to a hook in the ceiling, once there he took a rope from the nearby table securing her wrists in front before lifting them to the hook suspending her on her tippy toes then stroked his hands down the length of her body slowly smiling as goose bumps rose on her heated flesh. Reaching her ankles, he knelt before her sliding his hands back up to her knees, he pushed them up and out to slide them over his shoulders leaving her dripping pussy right at his mouth.

"Time to see if these lips taste like honey too." He said before running his tongue through her wetness.

The woman gasped and pulled against her bounds, but he just slid his hand around her thighs pulling her closer as he got started slowly taking his time to taste and tease every inch of her hot quivering folds, reaching her clit he lightly flicked over and over loving the little yips she was making, slurping at her juices that did indeed taste of honey. He finally sucked her clit hard gripping her thighs tighter when she tried to jerk away, and he sucked and sucked until she screamed her release. Smiling against her folds he began again licking and nipping at her folds up and down, over, and over making her jerk and yelp as her body continued to quake, and he had her cumming over and over. When she screamed again, he gave her one last long firm lick, and pulled away letting her legs come back down to the tippy toes as he stood.

The woman's head was back, and he could see the pulse at her throat as she panted. He smiled again stroking his hand up and down the middle of her body getting a throaty moan, and a gasping jerk when he pinched both her nipples rolling them back and forth between his fingers harder and harder than pulling slightly before releasing them making her yelp again. He then reached his hand behind her head he lifted it and claimed her mouth forcing her flavor onto her tongue making her take her pussy juices.

"Sire..." she breathed as he broke the kiss.

Marcus stepped back breaking all contact only to move around to her back and smack his hand against her ass.

"No words, or I'll gag that pretty mouth of honey." He said walking over to a rack of floggers and paddles.

Selecting a flogger made of brushed suede Marcus returned to the woman caressing her back with his hand before he started swing the flogger in a figure eight motion building speed before striking her low back and ass. The first two made her gasp some, the last of the next three had her yelping softly, the next six he increased the force behind them and had her screaming so nicely. Stepping into her body Marcus slid his free hand over her hip and across her hipbone before slipping his fingers through her wet folds playing with her clit, and when she came so sweetly, he bit down on her shoulder leaving a nice-looking bruise on her pale skin.

Marcus turned to the table at his side picking up another length of rope, next he looped it around her left thigh lifting it to secure it to the hook exposing her pussy fully to him. So pretty he thought petting her softly, nice light touches meant to drive her wild. Watching her rock on the toes of the foot still on the ground he kept a light touch up and down through her folds so pretty he thought again. He moved away walking back to the bathroom to get the bottle of whiskey. Lifting it to his lips as he returned to her, he swigged as he started to circle the flogger again striking her open pussy over and over watching it contract looking for something to grip, twelve more blows he took a last swig from the bottle. Setting it and the flogger aside he took his hard cock in one hand and her right thigh in the other he wrapped that leg around his waist as he slid into her fucking her harder and harder until she was screaming and convulsing around him. Three time he made her cum before finally letting himself fall jerking and shooting his creamy load deep into her hot pulsing core.

Breathing heavily, he pulled out releasing her and helping her over to the bed where he laid her out, rubbing some life back into her limbs before collapsing next to her and falling asleep.

2

Chapter Two
    Six months later

Bridgett was kneeling on top of a man, her wrist bound behind her back, and his hands were gripping her hips as he rocked his cock inside her core. Everything inside and out of her body was sore and tender. Bruised black and blue with red welts all over as well from the lords play over the last six months. He either used her maliciously by himself or shared her with friends beating her as they fucked her.

Tonight, a man was laid out on the hip high table with her straddling his hips, the lord had tied her wrists behind her watching as the man fucked his hard-thick cock into her core. When the man was seated to the hilt the lord bent her over the man's chest with an iron grip in her hair, and she screamed in pain as the lord struck her ass with a wooden paddle that had holes cut into it making the sting even more intense. Over and over the lord beat her ass and the man beneath her chanted more and yes over and over until finally he came shooting his hot load into her core. Seeing that the man had cum the lord dropped the paddle climbing onto the table behind her he thrust his hard cock into her ass fucking it hard until he came grunting like a pig.

While the two men were there huffing and puffing Bridgett stayed suspend on her knees aching with desire, sitting on the edge waiting and wanting to cum, but not allowed to. She heard the lord stop panting right before he pulled back slipping his cock out of her as he pulled her off the other man. She stumbled as he forced her over to a set of poles in the floor, unbinding her wrists only to stretch her out between the poles resecuring her before going to get a drink for himself and the other man. They stood there naked sipping on their drinks as they stared at her suspended shaking with unmet needs. She dipped her head closing her eyes. Suddenly a whip struck her abdomen sharply. She jerked and screamed. The man laughed in delight stepping behind her he circled the whip above his head striking her back with enough force to draw blood six times before he stepped into her licking the blood from her skin as he rubbed his hardening cock against the crack of her ass.

The lord stood there smiling as he finished his drink stroking his cock as it started to harden again. Now trading his glass for a crop, he walked towards her striking each nipple in turn, moving down he flicked at her torso with hard strikes working his way down to hit her clit over and over, moving to her inner thigh down to the knee then back up to her clit then down the other and back up to her clit. She watched his face grimacing when she saw a bit of drool seep from the side of his sneering lips before screaming as the man behind her fucked his dry cock into her ass. The lord then dropped the crop and fucked his now hard cock into her pussy, fucking her fast and hard against the man behind her. After they both came inside her the lord cut her free and the men man handled her over to the bed where candles where aflame around it. They petted and pawed at her body slapping, biting, and bruising as they got more and more excited waiting for their limp cocks to harden once again. The man then fucked into her pussy as the lord gripped her throat when he fucked into her ass. He fucked her over and over the bed banging against the wall no one noticed the candle fall, and the flame catch the bed curtain ablaze as the men lost themselves in a sexual haze. When the lord finally came in her ass, he collapsed atop her passing out from the sex and booze trapping Bridgett and the man beneath her so all they could do was watch as the room burned.

Hours later or was it days. Bridgett didn't know, she awoke surrounded by nothing but ash, coughing uncontrollably she rolled to her side and slowly got up walking gingerly from the room to find a simple dress and start making her way to Marcus's manor on the cliffs overlooking the sea.

Marcus sat in the back of the tavern with his little red headed toy on his lap. His mouth was sucking on her throat, her tits were on full display for all to see as he buried his hand in her skirts playing with her fiery wet fold. She gasped and moaned against his shoulder begging so sweetly for more. He loved her sounds, the quite ones and the loud ones. He wished he could take her upstairs now, unfortunately he had some business in town before he could truly play with her tonight, so he worked her pussy with his fingers sucking at her pale throat until she mewled so softly against his shoulder, and he bit down leaving a pretty bruise on her pale flesh. He then gently lifted her from his lap leaving her in disarray as he rose to spank her ass commanding her up to the penthouse as he left the tavern to conduct his business so he could get back to her and play.

Three hours later Marcus strolled back into the tavern swinging his pocket watch in circles whistling, his business in town had gone very well and he had a pretty little submissive to come back to. As he reached the top of the stairs he stopped when he heard a scream rip through the hall, and he ran. Coming through the door of his penthouse he froze when he saw the scene before him.

His pretty little redheaded sub was suspended in the middle of the room with her feet two inches off the floor, and another scream was ripped from her throat as something hit her back.

"What the Fu...." The man behind her came out of nowhere strike Marcus across the jaw causing him to black out.

Marcus came to strapped to a chair facing his pretty sub, seeing tear seeping from the corner of her eyes as the man behind her used what looked like a metal flogger to strike her back over and over. The man came around from behind her licking her blood off his fingers.

"This is what happens when you steal other people's toys." The man said as he struck Marcus's gagged jaw.

After retrieving a dagger from the table, the man returned to the woman. Starting at her left collarbone he slowly started carving little pieces of flesh from her body, working his way across to the right then to the center and down. Marcus strained against the ropes that bound him to the chair yelling and raging against the gag in his mouth. When the man reached the woman's lovely tits, he circled her nipples carving each one out in turn. The woman's screams now silent from the pain, and all Marcus could do was stare in horror.

As the man finished carving Marcus's sub ending at her shaved mound, he reached up freeing the sub only to throw her onto the table at her right. Strapping her back down he fucked her hard while licking the blood off her body. The man came jerking hard against Marcus's pretty sub hollering in triumph before turning and slitting Marcus's throat. Marcus died as the other man continued fileting the sub before stabbing her through the heart and leaving her there strapped to the table.

Two days later Marcus awoke slowly lifting his head to find that his sub had been stripped of all her skin showing only muscle, and he stared in disbelief. He breathed heavily trying to find some kind of calm, assessing his own body to see what was off. As he found nothing but blood on his body, he slowly worked his way over to the table collecting the dagger to start cutting himself free, he then said a brief prayer over his dead sub taking himself to the shower he cleaned up getting dressed quickly, and then went to take care of business.

Walking slowly down the stairs with a bag in his hand his stopped at the bar to talked briefly to the tavern keeper explaining what he would find in the penthouse and slipping him ten grand to clean it up without a word before heading out the door without looking back. It was time to find Bridgett, and work things out.

In the corner Conner stared ignoring the pint that slipped from his hand as a dead man walked from the tavern.

3

Chapter Three

It took Marcus three months of going from his various houses that he still held the deeds to before he found her. The sleepy little town sat on the base at the cliffs where the manor rose into the mist. starting in the local pub he found out that she had hired a butler and at least one maid to take care of the house for her, but mainly kept to herself.

Marcus knocked on the large wooden door with his heart pounding in his throat. Would she take him back? Had they had enough time to work things out? Would she even want to see him let alone take him back? The door was answered by an elderly gentleman who bowed formally introducing himself as Charlie, seeing Marcus into the parlor as he went to find the Mistress. Marcus scanned the room as he waited. She had changed some things since they had last been here, but not much, she had always liked the style in which his houses were decorated. How long had she been back he wondered walking to the blazing fireplace.

The years without her had been long and hard, but he would leave the choice up to her. He turned when he heard a soft gasp from the doorway, she was breath taking, was all he could think. Her sable hair was loose around her golden toned shoulders, and her green eyes shown with desire and hope. He smiled a small smile and started towards her.

Bridgett stood in the doorway staring at the man she had run from all those years ago. Why had she thought that he couldn't give her what she needed? Why had she thought she needed to do this alone? Marcus had always been there, from the first night he had taken her from that run-down tavern. He had taught her, loved her, and put up with her ups and downs over the years.

He still looked the same, she thought as he walked towards her, his jet-black hair just brushing his shoulders and his tanned toned skin was glowing as if he had been spending a lot of time in the sun. she smiled as his lips curved in a small smile of their own, and as he came within reach, she lifted her arm placing her palm on his chest. He was solid, and real, with a small sound in the back of her throat she threw both her arms around his neck holding on for dear life.

Marcus groaned crushing her against him loving the feel of her heat merging with his. Oh, how he had missed this just her body against his. It was heaven and hell mixed as one, pure bliss in his mind. Turning his head, he breathed in her scent loving it as he bit down on her throat, getting a sweet little gasp from her he slid his hands down her back gripping her ass inching her skirts up to her hips exposing her long legs before lifting her, so those luscious legs circled his waist and he ground his cock against her hot pussy. Oh lord, she was bare. He thought.

"Oh yes, more please." She moaned throwing her head back gripping his hair pressing his lips closer to her flesh.

Marcus smiled walking with her over to the couch he laid her over the armrest keeping her hips close to his as her upper fell back at that odd angle leaving her hips up, and open for him. Reaching up he caught the bodice of her dress pulling it down to expose her gorgeous tits, he played kneading and plumping them before squeezing them together kneading again and pinching her nipples twisting back and forth. The little sounds she made getting him harder and harder with her hips rocking against his, rubbing teasingly. Sliding his hands down he pulled back just enough to free his cock, gripping it hard he teased her folds rubbing up and down coating his tip in her juicy wetness flicking at her clit before going back down to fuck into her hot gripping core. Groaning he bowed his head in bliss staying still just to feel her squeeze him tight, taking a breath while keeping his eyes closed, he fucked her long and hard. Jerking hard he came over and over as she screamed her release digging her nails into his forearms in a deathly grip that left blood seeping from his skin. Laughing in delight he lifted her up carrying her over to the rug in front of the fireplace where he collapsed on his back with her on top of him.

"It's good to be home." He kissed her throat and stroked her back as they both drifted off.

Over the next few weeks, they spent most of the time wrapped up in each other making love or just holding and petting. It's as if they both didn't believe that they were back together. Almost five weeks after they had found each other again they were sitting out on the patio in the warm summer sunset listening to the crashing of the waves at the base of the cliffs. The table was set beautifully with a wine-colored tablecloth, candles, and dinner setting for two with Charlie bringing each course out in turn bowing as he left each time. The candles set around casting a soft glow over everything, Marcus lightly stroke the top of Bridgett's hand that lay on the table. When she turned it up and gripped his he smiled into his wine taking a sip.

"You have something on your mind, don't you love." He said circling his thumb on her inner wrist.

"I have an idea." She said taking a sip from her glass in turn.

"And what is this idea." He asked.

Bridgett grew quiet, staring at the table circling her wine glass causing the wine to swirl in the globe.

"Bridgett my love, what is it?" He asked trying to get her to look up.

"I'd like us to start a club of sorts. The club would be a bar and gambling hall, I'd also like us to start training submissives together auctioning them off for a night at a time to the highest bidder." She took a drink from her glass squeezing at his hand.

"Together?" Marcus asked watching her face closely.

"Yes, together." She said with a sigh and a small smile.

"Now there's a smile I haven't seen in a long time." Marcus laughed as he stood.

With his free hand Marcus set her glass aside pulling her up to hug her close stroking her back as he began to sway her in a slow dance.

"Anything we do from here on out, we do together." He said this as he nuzzled into her neck loving this woman even more.

"Always." She breathed gripping his back snuggling closer into him.

Over the next six months Marcus and Bridgett worked on setting up the club and finding submissives to train with Bridgett taking the lead as the dominate one known as the Mistress. At the end of six months the club had become a favored hot spot for the wealthy locals, and on the night of the first auction they had five subs up for bid making a total of one hundred thousand dollars.

That night had been the first night since they had come back together that Marcus had taken Bridgett as a submissive, tying her to the table open and exposed he pinched and teased her nipples sucking and biting grinding his cock against her folds backing away as she started to beg only to return with a set of clamps and a wand. Setting the clamps, he kissed her naval circling it with his tongue before setting the wand on low placing it lightly on her clit to tease and madden. Keeping the wand in place as Bridgett mewled and whimpered Marcus knelt on the table between her quivering thighs taking his cock with his free hand, he began to stroke it hard more and more panting heavily. As he came shooting his cream across her abdomen, he pressed the wand into her clit causing her to scream as she came hard straining against her bounds panting and begging for more.

"Yes love, always more." Marcus laughed standing up to unstrap her taking her over to the spanking bench.

Removing the clamps, he suckled each tit in turn soothing and teasing at the same time before laying her over the bench strapping her down petting her lovely body. before moving back to her upturned ass. Kneeling Marcus spread her cheeks and began slowly licking, flicking, and nipping devouring her pussy as if it were a dying man's last meal. He groaned against her heated flesh the first time she came, continuing his teasing as her juices coated his face smiling as she shrieked when he bit at her clit sucking it hard causing her to come twice, and licking up to her puckered ass he licked at it moistening the entrance. Standing up he lubed his newly hardened cock by rubbing it through her soaked folds only to move it up to slowly work it in to her pulsing ass loving the tight grip, when he was all the way into the hilt, he stopped letting her milk his cock with her gripping ass. God, she felt so good, his pretty little girl he ran a hand up her arched back taking her hair he pulled his hips back and thrust once, twice, and a third time had him cumming hard in her oh so tight ass. He grunted and groaned thrusting until she came gripping him even tighter. Pulling away he kneaded her ass loving the sight of his cum dripping from her back hole.

Walking away he went to their rack of floggers, crops, and canes, selecting a leather flogger he returned to her striking her lovely ass over and over keeping her mewling so sweetly as he reddened her skin making her drip even more. Changing his angle, he struck her pussy lips getting a lovely scream from her once, then twice, dropping the flogger he moved to her head fucking his hard cock into her mouth forcing her to suck until he came again. Now he unbound her carrying her to the bed and they fell asleep tangled together.

4

Chapter Four
Eleven years later

Bridgett's arms were secured to a hook above her head, and her golden naked body was on full and glorious display for Marcus as he circled her stroking, pinching, and spanking at his whim. She loved these times when she could fully let go of everything. There was no need for her to put on her masks that branded her the leader, the dominate one. With just Marcus present she could be his sub and let him take her wherever he chose, it was heaven and hell wrapped in one. The years fell away, and it was like it was in the beginning. Marcus hadn't known what he was back then, and Bridgett was so new and terrified after what had happened in her village that all she wanted was to feel safe and taken care of. Marcus had done that for her, taking her from that tavern and setting her up with him in his manor home. It was during this time that Marcus had taught Bridgett about submission and dominance, and though she may submit to Marcus whole heartily and there were times she needed it, she did prefer to dominate hence the ball gag he had secured at her mouth to prevent her from issuing commands of her own and forcing her to obey. She shuttered has he ran his hand up her back and gripped her hair in a vice like hold forcing her head back.

"You're so sweet when you submit to me love." Marcus whispered in her ear before biting down hard on the lobe.

"Now be a good girl and stay like this for me." His left hand spanked her hip before he released her hair with his right.

He watched Bridgett's whole-body lift with a sigh as she closed her eyes and waited, keeping her head back as instructed. Marcus took a step back and just stared.

Sometimes he couldn't believe this strong gorgeous woman allowed him to dominate her like he enjoyed doing, but even though they had drifted apart over the years, they always managed to find each other again. Marcus remembered when he had found her all those years ago. He had been sitting in the back of the tavern watching people come and go, enjoying a pint and a meal out of the house when she came in. He could see from her demeanor that she didn't know how to sell the services she was out to sell, weather it was an attempt for protection or just a need for a few coins, but each man she approached shrugged her off and sent her on her way. When she finally made her way to his table after finding no luck with the rest of the tavern, he pushed the chair opposite him out with a foot inviting her to sit. They had talked long into the night and when he had finally risen to leave, he accepted her awkward enticement for company and took her home, and that as they say was that in a nutshell. And here they were today many years later training subs together.

He placed his hands at her hips and gripping them gently before sliding his hand up her body, dipping in at her waist then flaring out over her ribs, and then push her breasts together and squeezing tightly drawing a low moan for her lips. He bent his head down and circled her left nipple with his tongue before sucking it into his mouth and biting down while his fingers pinched her right nipple rolling it not so gently between his thumb and fore finger. Causing her to cry out and jerk against her bonds. Marcus chuckled as he moved his mouth to her other breast and sucked it into his mouth, getting a low moan again when he bit down and pinched the other. He had learned over the years that Bridgett loved to receive pain as well as inflict it, and he felt privileged that she allowed him to see this side of her when, so few others did, but then again, he had trained her, and she always had been a good little sub for him. He suckled at her breasts a little bit longer then moved away to get something off the table a few feet away. When he came back to her, he had a pair of metal clamps in his hands, he pinched and played with her nipples again before fitting the clamps in place. He felt her shutter as he ran his hands up and down her torso, she was breath taking, perched on the edge almost ready to take that fall into blissful release. He slid his fingers down between her thighs to find her wet and ready, he stroked her folds with a light touch that had her thrusting her hips forward to try and find that firmer touch.

He chuckled softly and reached up with his other hand to remove the ball gag. "Now be a good girl and stay quite." He dropped the gag and slid his hand down the center of her body flicking at the clamps on her nipples as he went.

"Marcus......." Bridgett breathed.

"Fuck me now." She demanded.

"None of that now love; it's my turn to take control." He tugged a little harder on the clamp at her right nipple.

"Marcus make me come." She whimpered when he pulled his fingers away, then moan when he slipped them into her mouth.

"Tsk, I'm in control and I told you to keep this pretty little mouth closed. You going to receive ten paddles for each command you issue, you're up to twenty now do you want to add more? Or are you going to be a good girl." He whispered this in her ear and smiled when she began to shake with need. Pulling his fingers free, he stepped back and waited a beat.

She opened her beautiful green eyes and stared at him partly unseeing her need so great.

"Marcus." She said on a deep breath.

Marcus lifted an eyebrow silently daring her.

Bridgett quirked her lips in that way she had. "Marcus, I want you to shove three of your fingers into my pussy and fuck me till I scream."

"Oh, you do try my patience love, and I think that little smirk gets its own ten, so forty swats it is." He reached up and unhooked her arms, and then walked her over to the spanking bench removing the nipple clamps making a soothing noise when she whimpered before strapping her down and replacing the gag at her mouth.

Bridgett sensed Marcus standing beside her before he slid his hands from her shoulders to her ass gripping both cheeks and parting them to allow the cool air in the room to tease her too hot throbbing pussy then releasing her ass, he smacked both cheeks at once hard enough to move the bench forward about an inch drawing a scream from her lips around the gag. Would he count that as one...? or two? He had hit both cheeks dead center, and her ass now hummed from the impact, causing her pussy to plus even more clenching at nothing looking for relief.

A knock sounded on the door before Marcus could do any more causing Bridgett to lift her head from the bench and look at him over her shoulder.

"Stay here love." He said this with a wink as he went to the bathroom to get a towel; securing it around his hips he went to open the door.

"Yes." He said when he saw Charlie their butler at the door.

"I beg your pardon Sir, but there is a woman here asking for the mistress, and we can't find her." Charlie said.

"Show her to the drawing room, and I will find the Mistress."

"Yes Sire." Charlie bowed slightly and left without another word.

Marcus shut the door and walked back to Bridgett removing his towel as he went. "Well, it looks like we're going to have to cut our fun short. There is a woman here looking to speak with you."

His hand stroked up her back to gather in her hair and force her head up. "I should leave you in this state of need to suffer for your impish behavior, but I can be a selfish man and I have been waiting to come inside your hot core." With that said he positioned his cock and thrust into her fast and hard. Her desperate gasp around the gag turned into a low moan and her panting came in time with each hard thrust, he kept up a brutal pace until he felt her tense and then thrash against her bounds screaming her release, and he then let go thrusting once more then stilling before he jerked and came in her hot tight pulsing core. When he came down, he took a deep breath and went to work releasing her from her bindings, when he removed the gag, he gave her a deep gentle kiss wrapping her in his arms for a few minutes.

"Time to go back to reality I guess." Bridgett said with a sigh against his chest before biting down then pulling away to get dresses. "What did Charlie say?" She asked as she slipped her dress over her head.

"Only that there was a woman asking to speak with you." Marcus said stepping behind her to zip her dress up then gripping her hair in a tight fist pulling her head back.

"My impish little girl doesn't think this will make me forget that you have forty blows coming to that beautiful ass of your." He released her hair going to get dressed himself.

"Well, we best go see what's what." She shivered slightly at the threat, but in arousal more than anything, and headed for the door trusting him to follow when he was dressed.

Anyone who looked at Bridgett would see a woman that looked to be in her late twenties to early thirties, with golden skin and piercing green eyes that seemed to be able to find your deepest darkest secrets and fears. She had learned to be a confident woman over the years, and a large part of that was with Marcus's help he had showed her how to take control through dominance as well as submission and it had truly set her free to be the woman she wanted to be. But all that control almost shattered when she got her first look at the woman standing in the drawing room wringing her hand nervously.

No one but the male sub staring maliciously at Marcus when he walked into the room after the Mistress noticed the female sub in the corner staring deadly daggers at the stranger standing before the mistress.

5

Chapter Five

Two years later

Grace sat in the window seat of her tower chamber looking out over a raging sea. Thinking back to the day she first arrived at the manor house remembering that it had looked more like a gothic castle then a house of sin, as it was whispered of in town. Though her dress had been considerably modest she could still see the looks the town folk had given when she inquired about the manor. A place of ill repute they said, drinking, gambling, and prostitutes that do things no one should even know about.

She chuckled slightly now, if only they had known where she had come from. A house of ill repute was paradise to what she had left. Though her last Master hadn't been as curl to her as he had the others, the pain he loved to inflict was more than most could bear. She remembered watching as he used a barbed flogger on a disobedient slave.

"This is what happens to naughty slaves." He'd almost purred before landing another blow.

Grace had been five years old when her mother has been sold to him, and though her mother had shielded her from most of what went on in that house she couldn't protect her from the sounds that carried through the halls or even the next room when the Master had visited her mother. Grace also remembered staring at her mother's branded hip while she soothed the angry red welts the Master had left on her skin. The brand hadn't come from him, but from the training house her parents had sold her to when she had been younger than Grace herself a desperate attempt for survival in a world that was falling apart. And over the next nine years caring for her mother had become the routine, between the Master's visits and her illness, and by the time her mother had lost the struggle for her life, Grace seemed to go from the frying pan and into the fire. A week after burying her mother at the age of fourteen she had been escorted to the master's chamber by two silent slaves.

When she stood before him, he watched her face as he finished flogging the woman tied before him. When he finished, he dropped the flogger and walked to her licking the subs blood off his fingers with a dark light in his eyes.

"Strip her and leave." He commanded still staring into her eyes.

The two slaves obeyed silently then left, the soft click of the door shutting sounding like a gun blast in Grace's ears, or maybe it was the thundering of her pounding heart. Grace never knew that the sub left hanging there bleeding to watch as the Master took Grace for the first time was Lilith.

He then grabbed her chin and pulled her closer, running his thumb across her bottom lip.

"Your mother kept you safe from me while she was alive little one, but now that she gone you must earn your keep." His hand slid down her throat and he forced his tongue into her mouth.

Grace reacted on instinct blindly reaching up and scratching at his face. Gaging as the coppery taste of blood hit her tongue. The Master pulled away, spinning her around to grab the back of her neck, and forced her over to the bed.

"You'll learn little one." He said as he pushed her face into the bed.

"I rule this house and everyone in it." His hand came down on her ass with a hard smack, causing her to scream into the covers.

"Your whore of a mother might have made me promise to be gentle in your training, but you will learn if you wish to continue to live here." He said this while raining ten more blows to her ass, before flipping her over and tying her to the headboard before sliding his hands over her young body grabbing, pinching, and slapping as he learned how her body reacted.

Grace lay there silently with tears seeping out of her closed eyes. It should feel wrong, coming from this man she hated, but her body responded like her mother had said it would when touched intimately. When he pushed a finger inside her most private place she tensed and bucked at the intrusion and pain, trying to close her thighs. This at least got him to stop, though what came next, she was not prepared for. Ropes wound around her thighs, and they were forced open.

"Frist rule my little whore. You're mine and I can take you any way I want." This time when he entered her, he used two fingers and even though she was wet she still screamed from the intrusion, Master laughed as he pulled away again.

"You'll get use to my touch little whore." He said before slapping her throbbing pussy and leaving her tied to the bed, blindfolding her, he returned to the slave hanging in the corner. Grace lay there shivering as she listened to the lashing and the screams.

Two slaves had come later and untied her, but she stayed confined to her chambers, and over the next two weeks the Master had trained her, using other slaves, toys, and tools to teach her submission, all while never leaving a permeant mark on her, but for the nipple rings that all his slaves received when completing their training.

And then five years later the Master was dead, and at the age of nineteen Grace had to start all over again.

Shaking her head, she pushed that memory aside. The one thing she did enjoy from her last master's love of pain was the nipple piercings that he gave to all his slaves. She rubbed them now through the thin fabric of her gown, delighting in the thrill it rushed to her core. The polished steel rings were small with a green jewel hanging from them, and every time someone played with them or sucked on them it brought her a small flash of pain. The Mistress had marveled at the small hoops when she had seen them for the first time.

Grace remembered her arrival to the Manor, it had turned out that the Mistress had been looking for a new sub to train, and she had embraced Grace with the delight of a new challenge, though there had been a moment there when a look had appeared on the Mistress's face, and it was as if she had seen a ghost or something. She remembered the servants hadn't commented on her adornments when they had bathed her that day, they did their job and delivered her to the Mistress as instructed.

Not knowing what the Mistress wanted, Grace knelt by the door and waited after being led into the room. It had seemed has if she had sat there for hours, though now she knew it had only been but minutes. The apprehension and anticipation causing her breath to shorten, and her pussy to drip.

"I see you have been trained before." She heard from somewhere in front of her though she did not look up.

"Speak." The command came firmly.

"Yes Mistress." Grace replied without hesitation.

"We shall see how well in time. Now stand and let me see you."

Grace stood quickly keeping her eyes down and waited. Watching the Mistress's feet as she was circled, and then tensing unintentionally when she felt a hand caress her bare back, before relaxing into it.

"A new touch is always startling when you come from one who didn't treat you right. You'll learn to accept my touch, or you wouldn't stay, but for now there's time." And the touch came again with no tensing.

"Good girl." She whispered into Grace's ear and came back around in front.

A single finger started at her collar bone and sild down her body to her shaved mound, the light contact causing Grace's flesh to pebble and shiver. Then she brought both her hands up and gripped Grace's breasts firmly sliding her thumbs over her hardened nipples flicking the rings there causing a gasp to escape her lips.

"Sensitive, are they?"

"Speak." She commanded when Grace didn't reply.

"Yes, Mistress." She said

"Are they newly done?"

"No."

Mistress quickly released one of Grace's breasts and smacked her ass hard. "No what?"

"No Mistress." Grace replied quickly.

"Just sensitive then, it should make things interesting along the way."

She then moved a hand up and circled Grace's throat, not pushing into her windpipe, but squeezing the sides and pushing up against her jaw. Forcing her head up and her eyes to lock on the Mistress's, once there the Mistress stared for a long time. Then finding what she was looking for released Grace with a command.

"Go to the spanking bench and position yourself on it." She said this while walking to the sidebar in the room.

The spanking bench that Grace saw looked similar to a workman's sawhorse that was padded, it had four legs coming down from a board that was about eighteen inches wide and three feet long, set at each leg was another board that was about ten inches wide with straps hanging off them. Walking over to it Grace gingerly put her knee on one of the back boards testing the stability of it before bringing up the other knee and then placing her arms on the forward boards she waited. The padding was comfortable, but the position of her ass caused cool air to blow over her heated pussy making her want to squirm to find relief.

The Mistress watched her new sub kneel there obediently as she poured herself a drink; the ice clinked in the glass, probably sounding like bullets to the heightened senses of the sub. She eyed her sub as she poured the amber liquid over the ice, and enjoying the first sip she walked over, placing the glass on a table at Grace's side.

"Having been trained before you know that this is a balance of trust." She said circling the bench securing the straps as she went. Ending at Grace's head she tilted Grace's chin up with a gentle finger under it.

"The trust is knowing I will push your limits, but not break them. Do you understand sub?" The Mistress asked

"Yes Mistress." Grace replied quietly.

"But to keep that trust you shall be given a safe word, if at any point you want out say it, though know this if you ever do use your safe word, you will be gone from the Manor completely. Do you understand sub?"

"Yes Mistress."

"Your safe word is desert."

"Did you get that sub?"

"Yes Mistress."

"Repeat it for me one-time sub."

"Desert, Mistress."

"Good girl." The Mistress stroked Grace's cheek.

"Now I'm going to test your pain tolerance with several different toys. I need to see what you can take. Do you understand?"

"Yes Mistress."

"Good girl." Walking to the side Mistress caressed her sub as she walked to the table where several toys were lined up neatly. Choosing the soft leather flogger, she struck without warning landing a gentle blow on Grace's up turned ass, following with four other rapid, but gentle blows.

Pleased with her new sub Mistress gently rubbed the freshly reddened ass, putting the flogger back and picking up her drink Mistress took an ice cube from the glass and ran it over Grace's ass drawing out a gasp of surprise. Laughing softly Mistress slid it around and up to Grace's ass crack and let it slide down between her crack pulling a moan from her lips when it hit her heated fleshed. Then all touch and feeling stopped as Mistress stepped back.

She put her glass down and picked up a wooden paddle sliding the glossy wood across her palm before striking her sub on the bottom part of her ass, five quick blows and she was rubbing the red marks softly. Her sub took the wooden paddle nicely. Next, she picked up a thin cane, striking the tops of her thighs six times each, loving the red welts that rose on her skin.

"Good girl, you did well sub." She said gently as she caressed Grace's back before releasing the straps helping Grace to stand.

"We're going over to the bed." Mistress said wiping at the tears that had gathered at the corner of Grace's eyes. Then laying her on the bed she stretched her arms over her head and secured them to the headboard.

"You did very well sub, but we're not done yet." Saying this Mistress went to the foot of the bed and strapped down Grace's ankles and stroked her legs.

Moving her hands slowly up Grace's thigh she watched her sub's stomach tighten in anticipation, then loosen as she slid back down. Repeating this as she watched Grace's eyes dilate and contract before clouding with need. Sliding up one more time she parted Grace's wet folds to stroke and rub the swollen hot flesh, grinning wickedly as she watched the sub's muscles tighten and start to shake. Then she thrust two fingers deep into the tight channel and pumped fast and deep. Watching closely, she pulled out just before her sub could cum.

"Open your mouth." Mistress demanded before thrusting her dripping fingers into Grace's mouth.

"Suck them clean."

Grace clamped her mouth around Mistress's fingers as they slid in and out of her mouth cleaning them with her tongue. When she moaned around them Mistress pulled them out and grabbed her throat and took Grace's mouth in a rough kiss that stole her breath and caused her to wither against her bonds.

Grace whimpered when Mistress lifted her mouth and gently slapped her check.

"It's time to cum sub, are you ready?"

"YES, Please Mistress." Grace begged.

"Oh, you're going to be a fun one around here." Mistress said this before she set her mouth to Grace's throbbing pussy and devoured her like she was the last meal on earth; forcing one blinding orgasm after another till all Grace could do was whimper and beg incoherently.

Grace came out of her remembering panting with a liquid heat pooling between her legs slicking her thighs. Laughing to herself she could only hope that Mistress would come to her this evening. Rising from the window seat Grace began to pace the room, images flashing through her mind as the cool air teased her through the sheer silk of her dress.

She must have drifted off because when she opened her eyes again, she was no longer bound, and the Mistress was sucking on one of her nipples while caressing and pinching the other. The sensations it gave as she came fully awake were breath stealing, she went from a half sleep to a heightened achy arousal immediately.

The Mistress knew she had awakened for she slid her hand from Grace's nipple down to stroke her newly wetted pussy. When Grace closed her thighs around Mistress's hand, Mistress broke all contact, rising off the bed she stalked to the foot of the bed and grabbed Grace's ankles binding them once more forcing her thighs open to expose her pussy.

"Since this is your first training with me, I'll go gentle on you, but know this..." She said as she slid her fingers over Grace's swollen folds.

"You are never to close your thighs to me again, do you understand?" Ending that question Mistress slapped her hand down against Grace's pussy causing her to cry out.

Mistress watched her subs face for signs of distress, the flushed cheeks and parted lips that released panting breaths of need pleased her.

"Answer me sub." She watched Grace's mouth work open and closed, but only a whimper came out.

"Words sub." As Mistress's hand landed another firmer blow.

"Yes Mistress." Grace gasped out panting as a fire coursed through her lower body.

"Good girl." Mistress said as she smoothed her hands over Grace's inner thighs before unbinding her ankles.

"Now stand and face the bed."

Grace complied without a sound.

"Good, place your hands behind your back with the inside of your wrists facing each other." The Mistress quickly bound Grace's wrists with soft silk rope, when she finished, she stroked Grace's still reddened ass before taking her arm and leading her to the side of the bed. Once there Grace gasped when she saw the naked man gaged and bound to a chair.

"Gorgeous isn't he, and to think he has been there watching the whole time." She stroked Grace's neck as she whispered in her ear.

"His cock twitched and hardened as I paddled your ass, and saliva seeped from his gag as he watched me lick your pussy, wanting a taste of that forbidden nectar." She smiled at the man as she forced Grace to her knees.

"What do you think Marcus, is she one worth keeping?" Mistress asked as she stroked Grace's hair.

Grace watched as Marcus slowly nodded his head.

Mistress left Grace and went to stroke Marcus's face.

"Good boy." She kissed his mouth over the gag, then wrapped her hand around his cock and stroked up and down slowly.

"Grace you are not to close your eyes, you're to watch all I do to him. Do you understand?"

"Yes Mistress."

"Good girl."

Grace watched as Mistress sank to her knees and incased his cock with her mouth. She watched as Mistress's cheeks hallowed when she sucked before slowly pulling her mouth up and off making a popping sound as she released it. Then taking it firmly in her hand and pumping it hard and fast. Grace saw Marcus begin to pant around his gag making puffing noises with each breath. Then Mistress stopped, standing she paused a minute before raking her nails down his chest leaving angry red welts in her path, then running her palms up again she closed them around his throat as she straddled his lap, rubbing her pussy over his cock though not taking it in. Grace whimpered as she watched the ride, the slow angulation of her hips as they glided over him had Grace aching and dripping more then she had been. Then she heard the Mistress laugh. Looking into her eyes Grace saw delight in them.

"Well, well Marcus it seems our new sub likes to watch just about as much as you do."

Mistress laughed again before sliding back and taking his cock in hand to position it at her opening then with one hand still gently squeezing his throat, she slammed down on him with a moan of her own. Bringing the hand that was warped around his cock up to stroke his cheek she watched his eyes as she sat still with him pulsing inside her tight core. Then satisfied with what she saw she began to move taking him fast and hard, the slapping of flesh against flesh filled the room along with the panting of three people. A moan and a whimper escaped Grace's lips when she saw Mistress convulse and jerk against Marcus, then gasped again when Marcus yelled around the gag and jerked hard enough to move the chair and both bodies as he came inside Mistress. Next Mistress removed the gag and took his mouth with a hunger similar to when she ate at Grace's pussy.

Breaking the kiss Mistress stood up, and slapped Marcus across the face hard enough to split his lip. Though what Grace found the most shocking was she saw Marcus's cock jump and start to harden again from the blow.

"You see Grace there are different levels of pain, and different levels at which people can tolerate that pain." She circled Marcus as she said this running her hand over his chest.

"The pain of punishment is harsher than most, but that's how submissives learn, then there's the pain for pleasure, and that is where we test the limits of our subs to find that edge that brings a euphoric release that the body craves." She stroked Marcus's chest again with both hands stopping to pinch and roll his nipples between her fingers.

"The goal here is that tension you see in his face and muscles then watching it morph and relax into pleasure." Grace watched that tension and she could almost see the steps that he went through before she saw his body start to relax into the pain.

Marcus relaxed then shuttered when the Mistress released his nipples; and moved to grip his hair with one hand and run the thumb of her other hand across his lips gathering the blood as she went.

"Marcus here enjoys the harsher form of pain, as you can see from his reactions. And we shall test your levels later in your training." Mistress sucked her bloodied thumb into her mouth and closed her eyes in pleasure.

Grace watched in fascination as the Mistress teased and played with Marcus, but when she gathered the blood from his lip onto her thumb and suck it into her mouth Grace closed her eyes and shrank away even though she wasn't overly close.

Bridgett watched the new sub's reaction as she cleaned the blood from Marcus's lip and furrowed her brow in concern.

"Sub what did I say about closing your eyes?" She asked with a firmness in her tone.

Grace snapped her eyes open with a shutter and kept her eyes on Marcus as she answered. "To not close them Mistress."

Bridgett gazed at Grace for a long while before choosing to let the indiscretion slide and revisit it another time if it came up again.

"But for now, Marcus would you like it if the new sub crawled over and sucked your cock with those luscious looking lips?"

"Yes Mistress."

"Well Grace my sub, crawl over here and show me how you handle a cock."

With her wrists still bound Grace slowly made her way over the floor on her knees till she stopped between Marcus's well-defined thighs. Leaning down she started at the base of his shaft and slowly ran the tip of her tongue up his newly hardened cock tasting the flavors of both his and the Mistress's cum on it, coming to the tip she flicked the crown with her tongue before going back down and starting over. When she reached the tip again, she parted her lips and took his thick cock deep in her mouth bumping the tip against the back of her throat before clamping down with tight suction.

"Good god." Marcus exclaimed before Grace heard a hard slap and...

"Silence."

Then she felt the shutters before she slid her tight lips up then down again, loosening the suction as she picked up the pace bobbing up and down faster and faster panting through her nose, and when she felt him jerk slammed back down and sucked hard causing him to explode in the back of her mouth. She breathed in through her nose and felt the hot seamen slid down the back of her throat she tightened her mouth a fraction more swallowing as best she could before releasing him and sitting back on her heels with her head bowed panting, and a small bit of cum dripping down her chin.

The Mistress stood watching the sub's bowed head in awe, with her hands still resting on Marcus's shoulders she could fell his reaction to the girl, and in all the years since she and Marcus had been training the new subs this way, she had never seen a reaction quite like this one before. He was still panting and shaking for one. She gently kneaded his shoulders as his breathing returned to normal. The girl she saw was shaking with need and panting hard enough that with her head bowed her forehead almost touched the floor.

Giving him another minute, she undid his bounds, and kissing his temple she whispered in his ear. "Are you back love?"

"Yes Mistress."

"You did well." She said still rubbing his arms.

"Now go unbind our new sub and carry her to bed." She squeezed his arms and backed away.

Marcus knew Bridgett well enough that her moods could change at the drop of a hat so taking another couple of deep breaths he rose and went to pick Grace up. He undid her bounds without touching her skin, but when he went to pick her up, she tensed and shuttered.

"Hush now love we'll take care of you, put your head on my shoulder I'm just moving you to the bed."

"Please." Grace whimpered; she wasn't totally sure what she was even asking for. The need so strong, her nipples hurt they were so tight around the rings, her skin was so sensitive it almost hurt from the contact with Marcus. Yet she whimpered again when Marcus laid her out on the cool sheets.

Marcus stroked her face before turning to his Mistress who had a drink in hand for him. Taking it, he walked over and stretched out on the chase in the corner to watch.

The Mistress watched Grace shivering with need on the bed as she finished her drink, her hands gripped the sheets as she slid around trying to find relief, her skin was sheened with sweat and her breath was coming out in soft mewling sounds, the girl kept her eyes shut as if warding off or searching for something. Putting her empty glass down she went and laid out beside Grace, with her eyes on Marcus she ran her hand down Grace's arm whispering in her ear.

"Hush now, relief is coming." She settles her hand between the sub's legs rubbing ever so softly.

As soon as Grace felt that hand slide over her wet folds her body immediately contracted then convulsed with an orgasm setting her screaming as her upper body came off the bed before slamming back down. Now a mouth claimed hers and took and took as the hand continued to stroke and rub and pinch with a firmer pressure now drawing out the orgasm. When Mistress broke the kiss, she pushed two fingers in Grace's pulsing channel and pumped.

"Marcus." She commanded without turning her face which was now trained on Grace's, watching every slight nuance. Only removing her fingers when she felt Marcus's weight on the bed as he moved to position his once again hard cock at Grace's entrance.

"Now." She demanded pushing her fingers into the sub's mouth as Marcus thrust into her pussy and fucked her fast and hard while Mistress forced her to suck her fingers.

Grace exploded again clamping her quivering muscles around Marcus's thick throbbing cock until he jerked and came shooting hot cum into her core, and Grace moaned around the fingers in her mouth.

"She was denied a lot it would seem." Marcus commented as he pulled out and rolled to his elbow watching as she drifted into an exhausted sleep.

"I believe she has been." Mistress said as she stroked the hair back off Grace's forehead after pulling her fingers from her mouth.

"She has so much to give." Mistress said this as they both rose from the bed and embraced.

"Time will tell love." Marcus said grabbing her ass tightly.

"Leave her o rest and let me take you to bed." Saying this he forced his tongue into her mouth and walked her out of the room.

6

Chapter Six

Grace shivered coming once more from her memories, she never knew if that last part was something her mind had made up or if it has really happened, and in the two years she had been there she had never seen anything more than Mistress and sub between them.

After that night though they had both trained her over the next three weeks, and now two years later she was the highest bid on sub the Mistress had, doing most anything that was asked of her.

That of course was before she had been chosen as the Mistress's pet, being the only one of the subs allowed to wear the wine-red sheer silk that draped her body. Stepping back now she stared at herself in the full-length mirror. The silk flowed down her torso in two panels that barely covered her full breasts, and accenting the dusky nipples and their rings beneath, attaching to the skirt at her hip bones. The skirt was made up of two panels' front and back that connected at the hips with a silver chain that left the fabric gapping about two inches. Then finishing the whole effect was a silver chain that went from the two panels and linked together to run down her bare back holding the dress on her body. She loved the feel of the cool silk against her heated skin and shivered at the thought of Marcus or the Mistress removing it to play with the body it covered.

Marcus stood in the corner of the gaming room talking to their long-time butler that over saw the club as well as the house about the numbers for the night. From here he was able to keep an eye on all eight gaming tables they had running as well as the bar and its two dozen tables. When he scanned the room, Marcus saw the newer subs in their pale colored gowns or pants wandering in and out of the tables serving drinks or taking orders, smiling, and flirting with patrons that had been coming to the manor club since he and Bridgett had opened it six months into their training of the subs.

Marcus watched an older white-haired patron that had been coming since the beginning skim his hand up the back of a young sub's thigh under her barely there pale lavender gown to knead her round firm ass as she leaned over to serve his drink. The sub smiled at him letting him pet her for a bit more before moving on to other tables.

"Sire as I was saying the numbers are looking good tonight, there are plenty of guests indulging in the alcohol, and the house is up and looking to turn a good profit tonight." Charlie said after having to clear his throat to get Marcus's attention.

"Thank you, Charlie, be sure to touch base with the Mistress at the end of the night." With that said Marcus patted the man on the back and left the room trusting him to keep an eye on thing.

Marcus walked out of the room heading to his chamber to change before seeking out Grace.

When the knock sounded on her door she turned absently and went to answer it well looking at her back in the mirror as she went, getting a full view with her hair piled up as it was.

She smiled has she pulled the door open and found Marcus standing on the other side. "Hello..."

She didn't get the rest of the greeting out before Marcus closed a hand around her throat and took her mouth in a hungry kiss, backing her up and slamming the door shut again.

Marcus reached behind her with his free hand and broke the connection on the chain that held her dress in place causing it to fall to the floor and left her naked before him. He continued to kiss her until he felt her calves bump the bed in the middle of the room, where he broke the kiss and turned her to face the bed forcing her chest to the sheets. As he stepped back, he raked his blunt fingernails down her back ending with a swat to her round ass, before walking to her drawers to pull out a length of silk rope.

"Knees on the bed pet." He said walking back to her.

When she obeyed, he took her wrists and bound them behind her back forcing her shoulders and cheek into the mattress.

"Spread your thighs wider pet." He smiled when she complied. Then stepped back and stared.

She really was breath taking, he thought. Her milky white skin was flawless in its beauty, and when you add in the jet back hair and striking purple eyes you couldn't help but want to take control and lose yourself in her fiery heat. Walking back to the drawer he pulled two more items from it, and then returned to her.

He placed the items on the bed opposite to the side her face was turned. Sliding his hands up her thighs he kneaded and plumped her flesh working his way to her ass spending some time kneading it before pulling away, and then smacking both hands down on both checks ripping a scream from her lips before stroking and kneading again. Moving on he slipped a hand between her smooth hairless folds that were slick and dripping with need.

"Oh, surely we can do better than that pet." He chuckled behind her, getting a moan in response.

"What was that?" He pulled back and smacked her ass again.

"Yes Master." She whimpered against the bed.

"Better." He soothed the assaulted flesh.

Picking up one of the items on the bed beside her, he rubbed it through her wet folds coating it in her juices and then sliding it up to her tight back entrance then back down again before pushing it into her tight puckered ass then squeezing her cheeks when the plug settled nice and snug.

The anal plug that Marcus pushed into her ass was large and caused her to wiggle a bit to adjust to it. She loved it when any of the Doms used her ass, that tight full feeling that squeezes all the more when a thick cock was thrusting into her pussy, causing her to beg for release only to get denied and spanked creating a whole new set of sensations.

Marcus had been soothing her ass feeling it wiggle as she got use to the assault to her system. Judging it time he stepped back picking up the paddle and striking it across the jewel shining at the entrance of her upturned ass once, twice, and three times listening to her cries of need and desire, feeling his growing need as his cock thickened and twitched in his lose silk pants. He soothed the red marks before sinking his teeth into the fleshy curve of her left hip. Hearing her moan and feeling her push into his mouth causing him to bite harder sent a thrill through him. He stood then dropping the paddle and pushing down his pants before gripping her hair pulling her upper body off the bed as he thrust into her tight wet fiery channel and took her hard and fast.

Grace absorbed the feelings slamming into her system and let them flow through her like lava burning a fiery trail. The tightness of the plug, the steel like grip in her hair, and the hard thrusts of Marcus's hips drawing panting whimpers from her lips as she tried to hold back the building orgasm. It was heaven and hell all wrapped in a satiny vortex of need, pleasure, and pain.

Marcus thrust again and again, as he felt his climax nearing, he gritted his teeth and dug his fingers into Grace's hips and hair. Just. A. Few. More. And then.

"Cum now." He growled fiercely, sliding his hand at her hip down to circle her clit, taking her over that blinding edge of release.

Grace screamed as her orgasm took her over, blindly she peeked and fell into the abyss. She came back as he lowered her to the bed gently removing the plug, and releasing her wrist, rubbing life back into them and gently working her shoulders as he curled her against him to drift.

"Why do you play a sub... When you're so clearly meant to dominate?" Grace mumbled as she drifted down.

Marcus laughed softly again her temple. "You have no idea Gracie my pet." He whispered.

"Sleep now." He kissed her and hugged her close.

Marcus lay there staring at the ceiling long after he felt Grace relax into sleep. Stroking her back he let his mind wander. In all the years he and Bridgett had been together, apart, or training subs together he had never met a sub quite like Grace. She reminded him of the Mistress when he had first found her. She was everything a Dom could ask for in a submissive, though she had a mind of her own and challenged just enough to toe the line of punishment, and it was that that reminded him of the Mistress when she was younger. Grace still kept secrets that no one could seem to pull out of her, and she didn't seem to want to dominate like the Mistress did she was truly a masterpiece. True he did have his own dark corners that he kept from all but the Mistress, but for some reason he had this pressing desire to unlock all that this woman held inside.

He looked down at her when she stirred against him then settled again. He continued to stare focusing on the blooming hickey on her hips; it was a deep purplish blue against her pale skin forming into a flower of sorts. He loved seeing the marks he left on her, on any of the subs he took even the Mistress; they were like little signs that said for this amount of time they belonged to him. And at least to himself he could admit that it was getting harder to watch as Grace was sold to different Doms each time an auction was held, even though she wasn't on the block much since Bridgett had made her a prized pet.

His mind went back to the time six months ago when he had asked Bridgett if he could have Grace has his own. Oh boy had she beat him something fierce, he had been so black and blue he had been confined to his chamber for three weeks while he healed, but the way the Mistress had fucked him after the beating ...It had seemed like she had been consumed by a jealous rage that he had never seen in her. It made him wonder what had happened to her during their time apart. They had let each other go, because they needed to find out who they were apart, and in those years, Bridgett had grown and thrived, but something had happened to her that she wouldn't talk about. But there would come a time that he would pull the truth out of her, it was what he did after all.

Though their private relationship was vastly different than the one they presented to the subs they housed and trained, they were partners and had agreed long ago that whatever they did they did it together. But this time it was different. Grace was what made it different. Sighing he hugged her closer and drifted off himself.

7

C hapter Seven

Three days later Bridgett sat at her desk in the office under the bar going over the paperwork for the club. The numbers were looking good, alcohol sales were through the roof, the house was bringing in a good profit from the gambling, and the auction two nights ago had brought in close to two hundred thousand dollars.

She sat bent over the computer transferring the numbers on the screen into the leather ledger with her impeccable handwriting. She loved the convenience of modern technology that allowed you to keep track as well as transfer money with a few clicks of a mouse, but she still liked the back up of a written file.

Bridgett then wrote out the checks for their dealers and bartenders as well as Charlie, then updating everything and checking on their Cayman accounts she shut down the computer and stored the ledger in the fireproof safe.

Climbing the stairs, she came out of the office by a trip door hidden in the floor behind the bar. She stopped to pour herself a drink, and while sipping at it she wandered around the room. Absently skimming her fingers along the glossy surface of the bar, before weaving in and out of the tables.

The club was closed tonight, and she was holding a free play night, something she tried to hold once a week, a night when all their subs could play, but tonight there was something that had to be dealt with. One of their subs had been talking meanly of the pet her and Marcus had chosen, and mild reprimand had not work. So now as example must be made to quell any farther gossip Sighing heavily, she finished her drink, and went to get ready.

Grace sat at her vanity putting the last pin in her hair, tonight was a night that the Mistress held every week. A free play night is what she called it, a night where she gathered all subs in the ballroom that had couches, pillows, beds, and toys spread about, and she let her subs play. They could pleasure each other, or they could play with themselves, and the Mistress watched up on her throne so to speak with her pets, one was always Marcus, and for the last year and a half the other was Grace.

Sighing she shivered as she slipped a slim metal collar around her throat and secured it with a tiny pad lock. Staring into the mirror she stroked the cool metal, these where the only nights the Mistress required that she wear the collar. It claimed her as taken, though she could play with the others she was the only one of two who needed to gain permission to play. Marcus also wore a collar on these nights and needed permission to play.

When Grace entered the ballroom, she saw the Mistress up on her platform with Marcus lounging beside her his collar a thicker version of hers. When she scanned the room, she saw that she was the last to arrive tonight, the others were already lounged out playing or watching. The soft moans of early arousal sounding under the soft music that played. Aside from her and Marcus there where thirty subs in the house right now, ten males and twenty females all wearing different colors of sheer silk showing their level of training, the lighter the color the newer the subs. With her head up Grace walked to the platform and knelt on the first step.

"You're late." Mistress said this with disappointment in her voice.

"Forgive me Mistress." Grace said and left it at that, she knew the Mistress wouldn't accept any excuses.

"Come here."

Grace ascended the steps and knelt once again.

Marcus watched the Mistress's face as she stared at Grace, though passive he could tell she was looking to dole out a punishment, the set of her lips was firm and unforgiving, and the flash in her eyes meant trouble.

Mistress got up and walked to Grace staring down at her she could see the set of her subs shoulders as she waited. Reaching down she stroked her knuckles down Grace's pale smooth cheek before leaning down to whisper in her ear.

"Why did you not tell me what was happening pet? Have you not learned you can come to me with anything?"

She stood up straight again. "That you should have come to me with this."

With that Mistress walked off the platform and to the middle of the room causing all actives to stop. Her eyes scanned the room touching on each face before moving on. She knew she made an imposing sight, her sable hair was piled atop her head, her piercing green eyes lined heavily in black could seem to bore down to the darkest corners of your soul, her scarlet lips set in a firm line. The corset of wine red and black she wore pushed her firm tits together and up creating a nice resting place for the large ruby pendent around her neck, A jewel that Marcus had given to her when they had parted ways all those years ago, she cherished it more than anything she owned. The skirt she wore was jet black with two slits running up the front to end at her hip bones revealing her tones thighs, add six-inch stilettos and all her subs strived to obey her every command.

"As all of you know these nights are usually ones for the enjoyment of playing with each other, but I am afraid that tonight an example must be made." She paused as a collective gasp sounded through the room.

She didn't normally set examples in front of everyone like this. Punishments she felt were best done in private; after all it was well behaved subs you wanted to present to the public. But when one goes against all that their taught and then wants it to spread like a disease an example must be made.

"Lilith, come stand before me."

Lilith stood with a defiant look on her face and walked to the Mistress and locked eyes.

"I've done nothing wro..."

The strike came with no warning cutting her off mid word and splitting her lip with the force.

Then the Mistress had her by the throat and squeezed enough to have her eyes going wide and her breath gasping to reach her lunges.

"You have done something wrong, you insolent child and now you must learn, or leave. The choice will be yours after tonight."

Releasing her Mistress watched Lilith fall to her knees with a hand at her throat where red marks were already starting to form, and without taking her eyes off the sub Mistress spoke.

"Marcus bring the table, and pet turn around."

Marcus went to the side of the platform as Grace turned to face the room, and he carried a small table over to set it beside his Mistress.

"Mistress are you sure you want to do this?" He whispered soft enough so only she could hear.

The look she sent him was cold as ice and sent dread coursing through his veins. Sighing he bowed his head and began to back away. But one word stopped him in his tracks.

"Stay."

Mistress grabbed Lilith's wrist and forced her to her feet roughly binding her wrists in front of her. When she saw Lilith's, eyes go wide she spoke again.

"Marcus blind her."

"Yes Mistress." Marcus picked up the blindfold and went to secure it around the sub's eyes. That done he went back to stand by the table and wait.

Grace watched the Mistress secure Lilith's arms to a hook above her head and undress her revealing a pale torso with pierced nipples, and something niggled at the back of Grace's memory. Mistress stood there for what felt like an eternity before moving back and picking something off the table as she went. Grace saw Lilith tense then gasp as Mistress applied tight clamps to her peeked nipples. When Mistress pinched and rolled them between her fingers Lilith cried out. Then Mistress spoke.

"You defy me at every turn, is that what you believe subs should do?"

Squeezing harder. "Speak."

"No." Lilith gritted out.

Mistress stepped back and around smacking her ass.

"No what."

"No Mistress."

Coming back to Lilith's nipples she pinched them again, leaning down to bite the swell of the sub's breast.

"You try and convince the other subs to defy me as well. Then you talk down about my chosen pet."

Releasing the nipples again and moving behind her she raked her nails down Lilith's back leaving dark red welts in her path.

Reaching for the flogger she started a steady punishing rhythm; the sub was silent at first then started whimpering as the number of blows grew. Then one final harsh blow across her ass ripped a scream from the sub's lips.

"Who do you belong to?" She demanded.

"You Mistress." Another sharp blow.

"How do you act in my house?"

"With obedience." Another blow landed.

"What was that?" she growled.

"With obedience Mistress." Three blows came down.

"Better...What happens when you disobey?" Mistress asked changing the flogger for something else.

"I get punished Mistress." Lilith screamed when Mistress thrust a dildo into her tight wet channel.

Marcus watched Mistress fuck Lilith with the glass cock, thrusting it in and out over and over. He had only seen her like this once before, shortly after They had started training subs together. A young sub had been killed due to carelessness, and the Mistress had revealed a cold fury that he had never seen. Thinking back now that had been a swift punishment and banishment from the manor, but this, this was methodical.

Mistress watched the subs body langue and right before the sub could cum Mistress pulled the dildo out and backed away.

Lilith hung there panting trying to get a handle on things, she couldn't think, she couldn't process. The only thing coming to her mind was that that goody goody bitch Grace had said something. Grace seemed to be the goody goody everywhere she went, though Lilith doubted Grace knew they had been trained by the same Master. Then she heard Mistress's voice.

"Marcus stand at her right."

"Robert at her left." She called to one of the other males.

"Kneel." She said to both of them, switching toys again.

When they obeyed, she took Lilith's knees in turn and placed them on a shoulder, opening her pussy to the room.

"Grab her ankles." She commanded when Lilith started to squirm, and smacked her throbbing pussy with a paddle, drawing forth another scream. Putting the paddle down Mistress picked up a wand and placed it just close enough for her to get the barest of vibrations that left her panting and waiting for an orgasm.

Grace stared with a mix of sympathy, horror, fascination, and need coursing through her body, as the Mistress brought Lilith to the edge with a wand only to deny her that final fall. Over and over the Mistress did this as Lilith thrashed against her restraints screaming and mumbling incoherently. Finally, Mistress put the wand down and released the nipple clamps ripping another scream from the sub.

"Marcus release her and take her to the bottom chamber." She put the clamps back on the table.

"Everyone else back to your chambers, the night is over."

They all rose and exited the hall without a word. And in a dark corner of the room a male sub watched with loathsome fire in his eyes, thinking he had found himself an ally in his plan to end this rain.

Conner fallowed the last sub from the room watching Marcus release Lilith from her chains and carry her out.

When Marcus saw the male sub staring, he hardened his expression and barked a command.

"Back to your chamber."

Conner glared a moment longer before bowing his head and leaving the hall.

Marcus fallowed the male sub and watched him return to his chamber with a fuzzy memory in the back of his mind, before carrying Lilith to the bottom chamber, laying Lilith on the bed he lightly bound her wrists above her head. Then went in search of Bridgett.

Conner entered his chamber and waited twenty minutes before sneaking out of the manor to find a sweet young morsel to play with, the submitting shit was getting rather tiresome.

When Marcus found her thirty minutes later, she was lounged out naked but for the ruby pendent he had given her on a chaise in the parlor with a drink in her hand staring into a raging fire. He stood there and really looked at her, it had been a long time since he had had the chance to just look at her, and what he saw was breath taking. It had been decades since they had first meet in the run-down tavern, but she was still a site to behold especially naked. Her firm full breasts with their dark nipples that seemed to beg to be sucked on, her flat belly he loved to stroke, and the gentle flare of her hips inviting a man to grip. The brand on her left hip was a new acquirement since they had parted ways and he had yet to hear how she got it, but it only tempted him to lick and suck at her hip.

"Is it done?" She asked without taking her eyes from the flames.

"It's done with her wrists loosely bound. No touching for her tonight." He said this as he went and poured himself a drink.

"Are you sure this is a good idea?" He asked softly

"She's disrespecting the rules we set, an example must be made." She said this taking a sip from her drink.

"Or should I just have let it go? Would you have?" She looked at him then with a question in her eyes, before looking back into the fire.

He hissed slightly as he took the first sip of his drink and the fine single malt slid down his throat. Well, if you couldn't find virtue in the Mistress you could certainly find it in her impeccable taste for single malt scotch. Swirling it and taking another sip before setting it on the table by the wing back chair closet to her, he unhooked his collar setting it aside, and removed his pants before sitting down. She hadn't moved except for that turn of her head since he walked into the room.

"Bridgett what's eating at you love?" He asked softly.

Well that at least got her to fully look at him, as he watched her slowly turn her head.

"And what makes you think something's eating at me?" She asked.

"Not only do to the fact you went scary Dom on one of our subs tonight, but I also think it has something to do with why you beat me to a pulp six months ago."

When all she did was stare, he continued.

"I know Grace is one of the special ones, but why did a Dom asking for a sub, and a whiny greedy snotty sub set you off so badly?"

Bridgett seemed to think about that before she finally answered. And it wasn't anything close to the answer he thought it would be.

"For one, you promised that we would do this together when we started this house." She stared at him with a wounded look in her eyes.

And then she went off.

"She reminds me of someone Marcus, a girl I met in the training house I lived in shortly after we parted ways, but it's impossible." Shoving up from the chaise she began to pace.

"she was maybe in her mid-twenties when we went up through the steps together, hell she did just as well as I did when they taught us to dominate. But she looks the same as when I last saw her, and those purple eyes."

Turning toward him, she looked so lost. He had never seen that look on her face before. In all the times he'd dominated her and even the times he had gotten her to lose control completely, she'd never looked lost.

Even the first time he had seen her in that tavern, it was a determination to survive, not a lost helpless look he had seen. Even though he knew the lost helpless feeling was there.

"Have you tried talking to Grace about... do you remember the name of the girl who went through the training with you?" He asked as he stilled her pacing with a gentle hand on her arm.

"No, I haven't talked to her, she'd think I was crazy that was more than twenty years ago, and we didn't go by names they gave us numbers." She said leaning in as he began to rub her back in slow gentle circles.

His poor lost girl, would she ever get pasted that feeling of being left? Tilting her head up he took her mouth in a deep kiss, taking all her pain and distress on himself, while leading her back to the chaise. Laying back on the chaise himself he pulled her to straddle his lap. Starting with slow strokes up her thighs he worked his hands up her body watching her arch into him and purr at the contact. He loved watching her surrender, to give in to his silent demands, this fascinating woman who he had taught to control as well as let go, and when she trusted him enough to take her to the special place subs went, it was truly intoxicating. Kneading her tits, he watched her eyes close, and her mouth open on a low moan of need. Leaning forward he took a hardened nipple into his mouth and suckled it like a newborn finding his momma's tit for the first time hungry and greedy. Pinching and rolling the other between his fingers. Listening to her whimper and moan while she rolled her hips restlessly against him was making his already hard cock harden to the point of pain, sliding his free hand around to grip her ass he pulled her tighter against him circling his hips at the same time to slid against her soaking wet core. The moan turned into a whimper when he moved a finger to the tight entrance of her ass and teased, when her body jerked, he pulled his hand back and smacked her firm ass before biting down then pulling away from her tit.

"You know I think I've let you take control for too long my love, you're not getting all you need, and so tonight I'm in control." He said this as he rose setting her on her feet in front of him.

"Now my prefect little sub get your fine ass over to that spanking bench." He swatted said ass and walked over to the cabinet in the corner trusting her to obey.

Bridgett didn't really know what was going on, she couldn't seem to get her mind straight. It was all a jumbled mess of chaos and need. She knew Lilith's actions shouldn't have bothered her so much, and that Marcus would never go through with what he asked without letting her in on it all too. Maybe this is what she needed, maybe it was past time for her to let him take control for a while. So, she walked quietly over to the bench and positioned herself facing away from the cabinet he had walked to.

He pulled a handful of items out of the cabinet and then picked up his drink again before making his way to the bench, placing the items on a table just out of her line of site. Taking one more sip of his drink before putting it down beside a wooden paddle that had little heart cutouts on it. He then took his time walking around the table strapping her down touching, petting, and stroking as he went. Wondering, did he not convey his intentions right? Or were they really that far out of sync? They had always done everything together, since the first day he took her home. They had learned and grown together taking on lovers at a whim teaching them, fucking them. But it had always been the two of them. What had happened to his sweet and fiery Bridgett in their time apart?

Finished with strapping her down and back at the table near her fine ass he stroked his hands up the backs of her thighs, and gripped her cheeks spreading them wide letting the cool air hit her hot wet core before he bent his head and licked her swollen folds. He laughed against her flesh and repeated the path he had taken when she gasped and bucked again her bonds. Over and over, he continued his assault until she was whimpering and panting with need. He did one more slow sweep of his tongue ending with a flick at her puckered ass, before standing up and picking up the oil from the table as he went. Sliding a finger between her cheeks he watch her jerk again as the cold oil spilled over her heated flesh and as his finger became coated he slowly worked it into her tight ass coating the walls by pumping and rotating his finger in and out and around when he felt her relax he slid his finger free and picked up the plug coating it in oil he then began to work it into her ass, and when it finally slipped in he soothed her cheeks before bringing his hand down in a hard smack on first the right then the left cheek ripping a cry and a moan from her lips. He then worked his fingers back down through her folds to rub and pinch her throbbing clit, and when she started to wiggle and try to find more of something thrusting and grinding against his hand he pulled away and walked to her head. Gripping her hair with his clean hand he forced her head back and thrust his fingers wet with her need deep into her mouth.

"Suck them clean love." He said and fucked her mouth with his fingers, then pulling them out made her lick her cream off his palm before he leaned down and kissed her thrusting his tongue deep before pulling away again. Leaving her panting and whimpering with desire.

At her ass once again, he pulled an ice cube out of his glass and started drawing slow leisurely patterns on her low back and ass. He watched goose bumps pebble her skin, and shivers start coursing through her, and when the cube got just small enough, he let it slide down between her crack and melt on the base of the steel plug, causing the whimpers to turn into gasps.

"So pretty." He said stroking warmth across her back and ass.

"How many do you want love?" He asked kneading her ass now.

When all he got from her was whimpers, he pulled back and smacked one side. "Words, love."

"I don't know." She whined trying to arch into his light touch.

"I need a number...or would you like me to choose?" He said letting her feel the fullness of his hands.

"You choose." She said without hesitation.

"I trust you, take me where I need to be." She sounded so desperate and lost at the same time.

"Do you really love?" He asked sliding his hand up her back to grip her hair and pull her head back.

"Yes." She said on a breath.

Marcus made an absentminded noise before he released her hair and reached for the wooden paddle, and without warning brought it down across the tops of her thighs. Getting a scream from her lips. A second and third got gasping cries, and the fourth and fifth got low moans. When he replaced the paddle with the flogger, he got a whimper when he ran it up her heated red ass and across her back as he walked to her head.

When he got there, he left the flogger lying across her back with the strands spread and falling over her ass, then gathering her hair in a tight grip he brought her head up to stare into her eyes. And taking his hard cock in his other hand, he began to stroke it up and down nice and slow.

"See what you do to me love." Squeezing it just a little harder as a drop formed at the tip.

"Open your mouth and give me your tongue." When she obeyed, he slid his shaft along her tongue, coating it in her saliva.

"Do you want me to fuck your mouth love?" He asked when he pulled it out and let the tip flick the end of her tongue leaving that drop of flavor in her mouth when she closed it to answer him.

"Please." She said straining against his grip to get closer.

His hand moved from her hair to her throat as he crouched down and gripped her throat. "Please what?"

"Please Master." She gasped

"Good girl." He kissed her before standing again taking her hair in hand once more, and without a word placed his tip at her mouth and thrust deep when she opened for him and stopped. Then when he saw no discomfort from her, he fucked her mouth until he came in jetting spurts down her throat.

When he calmed some, he picked up the flogger and with his cock still in her mouth began a steady rhythm increasing the force with each blow, and as she moaned, whimpered, and gasped around his cock, he slowly felt himself getting hard again. On the twentieth blow when she shrieked around his cock, he pulled free, dropping the flogger, and releasing her hair he walked behind her again he gripped her hair and thrust into her wet pussy fucking her until she came over and over. On the third time he felt her convulse around him he smacked her hip and came with a jerk hard enough to move the bench a few inches then collapsed on her back panting.

Rousing himself enough finally he unlatched her bound body and pulled the plug from her ass then hauled her over to the chaise. Drifting off to sleep he held her close.

When he came to, he didn't know how much how much time had passed. Bridgett was on her knees sucking his once again hard cock, Stroking with her hands as she sucked the tip deep into her mouth over and over working him up until he jerked up thrusting deeper causing her to gag around him; that's when he grabbed her hair and forced her head back.

"You want my dick love?" He stared into her eyes for a moment, and then went on without waiting for an answer.

"Then we do it my way tonight. Put your hands behind your back." Taking his shaft in hand when she complied.

He guided her head back down making her take all of him deep as he helped her fuck him using the hand gripping her hair bobbing her head up and down, over, and over until he came again, but he pulled her back just before, so he came all over her golden tits.

"Crawl that fine ass over by the fire love." He said releasing her hair and leaning back.

He then picked up her forgotten drink and slowly finished it as he watched her lay there before him.

Finishing it off he slowly slid to the floor and stalked over to her, spreading her legs wide as he came up between them. With his eyes still on hers he leaned down and licked her oh so wet folds, flicking at her clit when he reached the top.

"Fucking hell." She hissed and her hips bucked up to meet his mouth in a hard grind.

He then released one leg and slapped his palm down on her pussy.

"No moving. Or do I need to bind you again?" He said this with the lightest of caresses to her assaulted flesh before positioning himself once more to lick and tease.

She hissed when he reached her clit again this time sucking it into his mouth, but she didn't move.

He felt her stomach quivering as he sucked on her clit rolling it back and forth between his lips before gently nipping with his teeth and going back down to start again. The fourth time he came back up to her clit and sucked it into his mouth he thrust two fingers deep into her gripping channel and fucked her until she screamed and started begging him to stop. That's when he came up her body and replaced his fingers with his cock and fucked her over and over until she screamed one last time, and he stilled then jerked against her as he came again.

Rolling off her and onto his back he pulled her to his side and stroking his hand over her hair said a single word.

"Sleep."

Bridgett felt the dream coming on but was trapped and helpless to do anything about it, when it crashed into her, she braced herself for what came.

The cell she was trapped in was cold and dark and she could feel the dampness on her naked flesh, would they come for her? What would they do to her when they did? This helplessness was nauseating, and the fear of not knowing what would happen to her left her fearing every little thing. The torture didn't really scare her anymore she was able to numb her mind to the pain, it was the comments and remarks that left her fearing everything the most. They say she was a witch, a descendant of the devil, but how and why, she had survived a plague, a disease that had killed most of the village and they condemn he to this torture for it. They came for her then strapping her to the table, the piously righteous men using her body as they sliced at her flesh with cold steel trying to purge the devil from her body with their cocks in ways, they never used them with their righteous wives, and with tears seeping from her eyes she sot oblivion.

The dream shifted; she was clawing free of a shallow grave surrounded by the charred bodies of the dead villagers. Then to the night she met Marcus in that run-down tavern. Image after image, them in bed, the first time he had restrained her, to the first time he had let her dominate him. Over and over the different stages of their relationship, till shifting finally to the time they had been apart.

Bridgett was bound in a line of serval other women and two silent masked men coming down the line, one exposing the hipbone of each woman while the other laid a searing brand to the flesh and if you talked or screamed you got backhanded hard enough to spilt your lip. When they reached her, she closed her eyes and absorbed the pain breathing through it.

"Welcome to the training house." She heard a short time later.

"You will be shown to a bunk and the number on it shall be what you're called, and your training will begin tomorrow."

Scenes from the training house flashed through her mind like a film in fast forward slowing as she watched the purple eyed sub leave the training house then flashing to six of the other subs' dead on the floor of the great hall, then to the night she fled the house of the lord she had been sold to and went to find Marcus again.

When Bridgett jerked awake Marcus was there kissing and stroking her, making soothing noises while rolling her to her back and fucking her until she passed out, back into the oblivion of sleep.

8

Chapter Eight

Come morning Marcus woke next to a cold hearth with Bridgett curled against him like a content kitten. He smiled, stroking her back and kissed the top of her head.

"It's time to move to our chambers Bridgett my love." He laughed at the moan he got in response.

"Come on love, you don't want the subs to find you like this now do you?" And with that he smacked her ass smartly, causing her to yelp and start cursing him.

"Come on now, up we go." He laughed louder as he hulled her up and into his arms kissing her soundly.

After putting Bridgett to bed in her chamber Marcus descended the stairs to the bottom chamber, with a glass of water and some toast. Upon opening the door, he found Lilith laid out on the bed with her hands still bound. She jerked violently when he sat down and ran his hand up the inside of her thigh.

"Hush now master's got you, just relax and feel." He whispered as he worked his fingers through her folds.

Rubbing and squeezing her wet pussy, he watched the tension in her face begin to relax as he brought her to that first rushing climax. Letting her pant, he reached for the water tilting her head so she could take a sip he watched her eyes open then close again as need took her. Putting the glass back he spread her thighs and began to lap at her pulsing core taking what he wanted as she withered, moaned, and screamed around him finding one climax after another. Before he thrust his cock into her tight hot pussy and fucked her till, she passed out. Then finding his own release he pulled out of her and left the room with the tray.

Finding his own chamber Marcus fell onto the bed and slept till noon the next day.

When Bridgett awoke it was to find herself alone in her own bed. She had a vague awareness of Marcus carrying her out of the sitting room, but her head was still fuzzy from the multiple climaxes and strange dreams from the night before. Rising from the bed she found herself stiff, and sore in places she had almost forgotten about. Stretching her arms above her head she moaned as her muscles pulled and calmed some. When she sat at her vanity she winced slightly from the tenderness of her ass, reminding her just how long it had been since Marcus had dominated their play, she had forgotten how much the wooden paddles sting lasted, or how many marks the flogger could leave on your skin. She sat there staring into the mirror as she idly ran the brush through her hair, thinking back on the night.

Though her treatment of Lilith had been harsh, she knew there was something the girl wasn't telling her, and she was beginning to think that she needed to have a serious talk with her. About this animosity towards Grace, and her future here at the manor. Putting the brush down she rose and went to her closet to dress, thinking something lose and flowy today so as not to irritate her still tender skin.

After dawning a dress of emerald silk that hugged her curve but didn't chafe at her skin Bridgett made her way down to the bottom chamber, pleased to see along the way her subs going about their daily duties. Walking through the door she found Lilith asleep, and the smell of sex in the air. So, this is where Marcus had come after he saw to her, she wasn't surprised or upset about; actually, she was kind of glad. Now with Lilith having found some relief they might be able to have a frank conversation. Reaching out she unhooked the cuffs holding Lilith's wrists then waited as the girl woke up, when Mistress saw she was fully awake she spoke.

"Sit up." She commanded softly.

When Lilith complied, Mistress reach around and secured her wrists behind her, and went to the chair in the corner of the room.

"Now my dear we need to have a conversation." Mistress said as she took a set.

"Now we need to talk." Lilith said with a scoff of disgust in her voice.

"Yes." Mistress said.

When Mistress left it at that Lilith began to wonder and start to squirm a little. Finally breaking the silence.

"And what do we need to talk about?" She started.

"You've already made your feelings clear.... and to the entire house on top of it."

"Is that what you feel I did last night." The Mistress said

"Speak." She commanded when it was met with silence.

"Yes."

"Yes, Mistress." Lilith tried again when she saw The Mistress just raised an eyebrow at her.

"Well, it's good to know that you do eventually learn." Mistress said.

"What I did last night was express my displeasure at vindictive gossip, while setting an example for any who would think to fallow in your footsteps with it."

"And what I need now is for you to explain to me your displeasure and venom towards Grace. The truth, not what you think I want to hear or only what you want to give, I want it all."

The Mistress stared at her for a long time while she gathered her thought. Could she do this? And what would happen to her if she did, and the Mistress didn't like it? Now that she thought on it, it was a little petty. Taking a breath, she began.

"Grace and I had the same Master?" She said.

"I gathered that much when I saw your piercings, what does that have to do with this venom?" Mistress asked when Lilith paused.

"The Master...He was cruel, he liked the harsh pain of punishment. He'd make you bleed just so he could lick it from your skin, and then leave you after to see to yourself, and it wasn't just the slaves who disobeyed but all of them."

"Slaves?" The Mistress asked quietly.

"That's what we were, not subs, but slaves. There for him to use, discard, trade, and torment at his whim. But he never treated Grace like everyone else, it was almost like she was precious to him, even though he made her watch everything he did to the others." Lilith paused with her head bowed.

Mistress watched her for a long time before speaking.

"Did you ever thing that maybe that was worse?" She asked

"More psychological than physical. Sometimes that leaves a mark harsher than any punishment."

Lilith looked up at the Mistress then with a seeking look.

Mistress laughed softly. "Don't go looking for my past sub, it's a book you're not ready to read."

Lilith bowed her head again.

"So, what's to happen to me?" She asked quietly.

"I told you last night my dear, that starting today it would be your choice."

"But it also means you're going to have to start changing your attitude." Mistress said this with a pointed look.

"You still have some consequences coming because of your actions, and I'm still thinking on some things, but you can stay as long as you start obeying better and stop spreading gossip."

"Thank you, Mistress." Lilith kept her head bowed

"Now I think it's time to get you cleaned up." Mistress rose and took Lilith by the upper arm and lead her into a bathroom that had a large shower without anything blocking the view, and a padded bench along one wall. And Mistress removed the cuffs and whispered one word.

"Go."

So, Lilith walked into the shower and turned it on to bathe with the Mistress watching. She flinched slightly as the cold water hit her skin causing her nipples to harden, and then relax into it as the water warmed caressing her skin lulling her into bliss. Picking up the soap she began to lather her body stroking, squeezing, and kneading as she went. When her hands slid down between her thighs, she received a harsh command.

"Do not make yourself come subs."

She rubbed once then twice with soapy fingers sliding through heated arousal, before taking her hands back up her body to knead her tits. Putting on a show for the Mistress.

"Enough." This came as Lilith started to flick at her nipple rings.

"Finish up cleaning yourself then go lay on the bed."

Lilith stroked her body one final time before rinsing off the soap, then taking a towel to dry herself on the way back to the bed.

Bridgett sat in the bathroom a while longer as she listened to the sub settle on the bed. Her head was still in a somewhat fragile state, she probably shouldn't even be down here playing this game, but she'd finish what she started so rising she went to the counter and found the scented coconut oil and went out to do some teasing of her own. Stopping to pull a blindfold out of the drawer as she passed it.

When she came out of the bathroom, she found Lilith stretched out on the bed with her arms above her head waiting.

"Roll over into your stomach sub."

When she complied, Mistress crawled onto the bed and straddled her thighs. Mistress first took Lilith's arms and brought them down by her sides, then reached up and wrapped the blindfold around her eyes sending her into darkness. Moments later she felt the warm drizzle of oil down the center of her back, followed by Mistress's hands as she worked the oil slowly over her skin, gently working and kneading the muscles of her back working her way down to Lilith's plump ass. Kneading and playing with it till Lilith began to squirm, then Mistress lifted her hands and smacked them down hard leaving two red hands prints on Lilith's cheeks.

"Don't move." The Mistress said, repositioning herself at the sub's feet.

She poured more oil over her legs, and then gently rubbed it in working down to her feet.

"Roll over."

When Lilith rolled onto her back the Mistress started to work the oil into and up her legs parting them as she went to start teasing her finger through the sub's wet folds, slipping, and sliding along drawing moans and whimpers from lips parted in need. Then she bent her head and followed her fingers with her tongue starting the teasing anew, when Lilith began to squirm Mistress stopped and continued her massage up the sub's torso. At her tits Mistress squeezed them tightly together and flicked at a ring with her tongue watching the nipple pebble and harden to a stiff peek before sucking it into her mouth, as Lilith began moving restlessly again Mistress moved on to repeat the process with the other one, and when she got the same reaction, she then started massaging her way over the sub's chest and up to her shoulders and throat. After a short time teasing her way around her throat, she moved on to her arms working first one then the other before sliding back up to her throat nuzzling gently before biting down hard feeling the sub jerk beneath her. Laughing she broken all contact and got off the bed, walking back over to the set of drawers took a chastity belt from it and went to secure it on Lilith.

"You'll wear this until I see fit to remove it." Mistress said removing the blindfold and stared as Lilith blinked against the soft light in the room.

"And you'll stay here until I say as well."

"Answer me sub." Mistress said when there was no reply.

"Yes Mistress."

"Good, someone with be along with some food later today." And Mistress left the room.

Without looking back Bridgett closed the door and went looking for Marcus, though the night before had helped she could still feel the chaos building in her head, and she still needed to figure things out. She still needed to talk to Grace and figure out what to do about Lilith. But she couldn't seem to get her head on straight; it was like she got a thought and then lost it again within minutes. Maybe Marcus could help her. He had always been able to ground her, to clear all the crap from her head. That was what learning to submit had done for her, and it seemed that she had been dominating others too long.

When she reached Marcus's chamber, she found him asleep. So instead of waking him she went and found some paper and a pen to leave him a note. With that done she went to the room at the back of his chamber and knelt on a padded bench to wait.

9

Chapter Nine

Marcus awoke the fallowing day to the note laying on his nightstand next to his head and reading it he rose from his bed and went directly to the back room to find Bridgett kneeling on a bench facing away from the door. Walking silently over to her he knelt behind her with his thighs hugging the outside of her claves and wrapped one arm around her middle just under her breasts and the other hand gently around her throat.

"How long have you been sitting like this love?" he whispered the question against her ear.

"I don't know...What times is it?" she asked just as quietly.

"It's mid-day, the day after I put you to bed in your chamber." He said this before sucking her lube into his mouth.

"Then I've been here for twelve hours, maybe more I don't really know." She replied on a sigh.

He drew back from her then.

"Twelve hours?"

"Why in the hell did you not wake me?" he demanded releasing her to stand before gripping her upper arm to make her stand with him.

She stumbled and fell against him when she gained her feet, and he swept her up into his arms and carried her to the bed with a fierce growl.

"Answer me, Bridgett." He barked standing over her, after laying her out on the bed.

She still didn't answer him, she lay there with her eyes closed breathing deeply. She still couldn't think straight, what she needed to do and what she wanted to do, the questions she had and the answers she'd received where all jumbled up in her head and she couldn't sort them out. Did she need to submit, or did she need to dominate? All she knew at the moment was that she needed Marcus.

"Bridgett love.... I asked you a question. You need to answer me now." He said this with a heavier command in his voice.

"I needed to think.... You needed to sleep." She whispered

"My need to care for you is much greater then sleep love, and maybe it is that you think too much or too hard. It may be time to shut it off for a time."

Marcus reached down and picked her up again carrying her over to a massage table in the corner after laying her on it he commanded her to roll over onto her stomach. Taking a bottle of oil off the nearby table he began working it over her back, slowly going up and down over and over in nice gentle strokes before circling the table and starting on one of her legs, he slowly worked his way around her body gradually feeling her body go lax, and then told her to turn over onto her back and started the process over again. Working up her legs but avoiding the junction between her thighs and moving on to circle her stomach and moving up to knead her breasts, watching her arch her back into his touch and moan at the contact. And when she went pliant under his hands, he slid them up to her throat and kissed her parted lips.

Picking her up once more he carried her over to the spanking bench and placed her on it. Walking around he strapped down each of her limbs before rounding back to her ass, stepping to one side he smoothed his hands over her golden skin, leaving one sitting at the small of her back and the other over her curved cheeks, listening to her breath hitch and start panting out as he started smacking in a slow steady rhythm. First one cheek then the other over and over, and back and forth, her panting breath turned into gasps and moans. As he felt her start to shutter, he took his hand smacking her ass, before sliding two of his fingers between her wet folds working them in and out, and up to her clit to circle it firmly stroking his hand on her back up to her hair to grip hard forcing her head back as her moans turned into whimpers. And finally thrusting his fingers deep inside her hot pussy fucking her until she screamed and thrashed against her bonds.

When she settled down, he started all over again setting a slow rhythm on her ass and spanking her till she was on the brink of cuming and letting her settle before teasing her till she was on the brink again and then finger fucking her till she screamed and came. And he repeated this until she passed out and then carried her back to the bed and let her sleep. Leaving her be he went and gathered the subs to tell them that the Mistress would be unavailable for the time being and that they were to continue with their daily tasks and stay confined to their chambers at night till father notice, he also checked in with Charlie making sure that the club and the house were running smoothly.

10

Chapter Ten

Over the next three weeks Marcus kept Bridgett in his personal playroom and used her as he saw fit. Taking her to the edge and denying her the fall again and again, then fucking and spanking or flogging her until she passed out. And it was those times that she slept deeply that he made his rounds checking in with Charlie, making sure the subs were doing what they were supposed to be doing. He would also go check on Lilith, and though he kept her in a heightened state with the chastity belt on he left her unbound.

Three weeks later Marcus was lying in bed with Bridgett curled against him, He knew she wasn't sleeping but he continued to just stroke her hair and lay there in a peaceful silence. Waiting, He knew she had something to say, He could see it every time the fog cleared from her eyes over the last few days, she was finally getting her head wrapped around whatever it was she needed to figure out.

Bridgett lay there feeling Marcus's hand travel up and down her back, slowly and gradually she had felt herself centering again, and the thoughts in her head realigning so she could process them, and figure things out. This is what she had missed when they had been apart all those years. The ability to go to him and find that centering of her mind and the inner peace that allows her to figure things out.

"Lilith told me her story." She said finally feeling his hand pause midway up her back.

"And what was her story?" Marcus asked gently.

"She told me about the Master that trained both her and Grace. She said that he was a cruel man that used slaves instead of training subs, and her hate comes from her seeing that man go easier on Grace then every-one else.”

“And what did Grace have to say about that when you talked to her?”

She was quite at that question, and to him her silence spoke volumes.

“You haven’t spoken to Grace, have you?”

“I couldn’t find the way of how to talk to her.” She said against his chest.

“I couldn’t think straight, I needed you more then I needed to talk to Grace at the time.”

“And you feel that now you’re ready to talk to her, do you?”

Bridgett sat up and straddled Marcus’s hips. Sliding her wet fold over his hard cock.

“I think I am, but I think I need to play with some of my subs first.” And with that she thrust onto him taking him deep inside and fucking him till they both came hard.

After showering and pulling on a lose dress Bridgett marched through the halls with a single purpose and reaching the first door knocked. When it was answered she spoke two words.

“Playroom now.”

Then went to two other doors and repeated the same two words.

When she got to the playroom, she found the three of her male subs kneeling on the floor waiting for her. She stood there for a moment and looked at them kneeling there with their heads bowed and glanc-ing to the corner she locked eyes with Marcus who was lounging on a chaise with a smug smile and a drink in his hands. And with his nod of encouragement, she turned back to her task. All three of her subs were good looking men, two of them had dark chestnut brown hair that hung down to just brush their shoulders; and the other had jet-black hair that was shorter but there was a front wave that fell over his brow to hang in his eyes.

Walking over to the table at the side of the room she picked up serval items before walking behind the trio of subs. Calmly she blindfolded each one in turn and secured a collar around Alec's throat and stroked his chestnut locks before urging him to stand silently by pulling on the leash attached to the collar.

She led him over to where a series of hooks hung from the ceiling, she then bound his hands and put them over the hook above his head detaching the leash. She stroked his chest up and down, petting him like a prized stallion. Sliding her hand lower she gripped his cock firmly pumping up and down listening as his breath shortened with each stroke. Releasing him she circled around to his back trailing her fingernails across his skin causing him to shutter, up and down his back she smiled when she heard the low moan and broke contact.

Walking over to Marcus she gripped his hair and thrust her tongue into his mouth in a fierce brief kiss before walking to the rack that held the floggers, choosing one she went back to Alec and began a forceful rhythm up and down his back and over his firm ass. The welts bloomed quickly and got darker and darker, making her smile. Circling around she struck his hip before kneeling down and sucking his cock into the back of her throat with a hard suction, bobbing her head up and down quickly bringing the sub to the edge then standing before he could cum stepping back, she struck his chest repeatedly with the flogger, then gripping his throat she kissed him hungrily as she squeezed. Breathing heavily, she unhooked his hands and lead him to a hip high table stretching his hands across the table, looping the rope over a hook set at the end. Stroking the welts on his back she moved back to his ass striking it hard.

"Spread your legs sub." She said staring over at Marcus as the sub obeyed.

Walking to another table she picked up three items and went back to grip his cock between his thighs pumping hard enjoying the feel of him hardening even more at her touch. Releasing him she slid her fingers up through his ass crack circling his puckered hole, then gripping his cheeks and kneading them before reaching over for the bottle of lube she had set beside him, opening it she squeezed a stream of clear oil out and watched it run down his open crack. Putting it back down she picked up the anal plug rubbing it through the oil to coat it before slowly pushing it into his tight hole.

"Relax." She cooed rubbing his back after the plug was seated snuggly in his ass.

She felt him shutter as he adjusted to the intrusion then when she had felt him calm, she picked up the paddle and beat his ass over and over. And when her breath was panting out of her chest, she stepped to the top of the table releasing his hands and pushing him up and into a chair straddling him she re-secured his hands behind the chair and fucked him like a woman possessed, over and over she pounded him feeling him shaking with the need to cum. With her muscles tightening around him she whispered in his ear.

"Cum."

Shuttering when he released inside of her, she let herself cum screaming as she dug her fingers into his shoulders.

Getting off him she went over to Marcus and knelt beside him to suck his hard cock into her mouth and sucked him until he jerked with a hiss and came in her mouth. Wiping at the drop of seamen at the corner of her smiling mouth she stood, kissed his smiling mouth, and went to release the sub removing the plug and lead him over to kneel in the corner.

"Now listen as I fuck the others just the same." She whispered licking at his ear before walking over to the other subs.

She repeated this release of tension with the other subs fucking Marcus with her mouth after each one, and when Conner bagged her to stop, she slapped him across the face hard enough to spilt his lip. But when she finished blowing Marcus the third time, he grabbed her hair and forced her to look at him, bringing her slowly up to whisper in her ear.

"What are you playing at love?" He whispered.

"Not at love, with." She said nipping at his chin.

"Now I'm going to get our two girls to play along."

Marcus sighed and released her hair. "Fine love, go get our girls to play with."

Marcus quirked his eyebrow at Bridgett when she returned with Grace and Lilith, but Lilith was gagged.

"We don't want the audience talking during the show now do we love." She pecked his lips with hers while sitting Grace by him and taking Lilith over and binding her to a chair so she could watch all the play.

Going over to the three subs in the corner she removed their blindfolds and pulled Conner up with a fist in his hair and forced him into the chaise across the room, binding him to it.

"Grace mount him now." She went back to the subs without seeing if she obeyed.

She came back with Alec in tow. "Put your cock in her ass." Saying this she spread Grace's ass and poured oil down the crack before coating her palm to slick his cock and guide it in, then bound his hands behind him.

Going back for Robert, she pulled him in front of Grace, while binding his hands behind him.

"Pet suck his cock into the back of your throat." She stepped back when Grace complied.

"Now freeze."

"Look Lilith, isn't it perfect?" She looked at her gagged sub.

"A breath-taking site, do you know why I chose Grace as my pet?" She asked.

Lilith shook her head since her mouth was non-useable.

"It's because she'll let me do anything to her with total trust." Mistress stroked Lilith's hair and walked back to pick up the oil before going to Marcus and slicking his cock with her oiled hand. Kissing him firmly before issuing a command.

"Go fuck Robert's ass pet." She turned and watched.

Marcus walked over to Robert and ran his hand across his lower back and over his reddened ass feeling him tense under his hand.

"Hush now, you know how this feels, just relax."

He took his cock in one hand and spread Robert's ass with the other and slid in nice and slow stopping every few inches to let him get use to the feeling.

When he was all the way in, he stopped and waited.

"Marcus...Fuck him." The Mistress's voice was firm and commanding.

Marcus took a deep breath watching Robert breath with him he ran his hand over Roberts back as he began to move fast and hard pounding over and over. When he felt Robert tense, he leaned forward and bit his shoulder hard listening as Robert yelled his release into Grace's mouth.

"Marcus pull out and come here."

"Robert go kneel in the corner."

Marcus pulled out of Robert and walked over to the Mistress and knelt. Robert went and knelt in the corner with his head bowed.

"Stand up and go fuck Alec's ass." Mistress stroke his hair as he stood and walked behind Alec, slicking his cock with another coat of oil on the way.

Stroking Alec's back Marcus thrust into his ass when he didn't sense any hesitation and fucked him fast and hard. When Alec screamed his release into Grace's ass Marcus pulled out and went to his Mistress and waited.

Mistress stroked a hand over Marcus's face.

"Alec go kneel in the corner, Grace my pet go lay on the bed."

Grace rose off Conner's throbbing cock and went and laid back on the bed, while Mistress removed the blindfold and unbound Conner, but placed a chastity device on his stiff cock then told him to kneel in the corner. Mistress then walked to Lilith and unbound her.

"Not a word." It was a firm command as Mistress removed the gag.

"Marcus come with us." Mistress said walking to the bed with Lilith.

"Play with her sub." Mistress commanded pushing Lilith to get up on the bed.

Lilith ran her hands up Grace's body when Mistress lifted Grace's arms above her head looping the ropes on the headboard around them as Lilith started stroking, rubbing, and pinching.

"Her pussy is waiting Marcus, and I think it's needy" She chuckled and smack his ass as she watched Lilith take one of Grace's nipples and sucked it into her mouth.

Marcus climbed onto the bed between Grace's thighs thrusting deep when she cried out as Lilith bit down on her nipple while pinching the other. Marcus began to move faster but got a command from Mistress.

"Slow down Marcus, I want her to feel it all."

" Lilith Straddle Grace's waist and take her mouth with yours."

When Lilith obeyed, Mistress gave another command.

"Marcus speed up now."

She watched as Grace was consumed with need, desire, and sensation.

"Marcus stop." Mistress commanded.

"Lilith break the kiss and put your oh so wet pussy over Grace's mouth."

Lilith broke the kiss and looked at the Mistress sharply.

"Lilith." Mistress arched a brow. And Lilith obeyed.

"Good, Marcus hold Lilith's arm behind her.... Now finishing fucking Grace while she licks Lilith off."

Mistress watched the show as she listened to Marcus's balls slapping against Grace, and Grace slurped up Lilith's juices, and Lilith began to moan and whimper.

"Cum now...all three of you." And she smiled as the sound echoed around the room.

After they calmed down some, Mistress walked to them gripped Lilith's hair commanding Marcus to release her and lay next to Grace and pulled Lilith off the bed.

"Stay." She ordered to Lilith as she herself climbed between Grace's thighs, first kissing Grace deeply sucking Lilith's flavor from Grace's mouth, then sliding down to flick at her nipples before continuing down to lick Marcus's cum from Grace's pussy. Licking, sucking, and nipping until Grace was panting and whimpering, and let her fall over and over. She then shifted positioning her pussy at Marcus's mouth getting him to start licking at her before sucking him deep into her throat with a hard suction, and when she felt herself start to cum, she sucked harder getting him off as she creamed his face with her orgasm.

"Subs to your chambers." She commanded as she shift to lay out on the side of Grace that was empty cocooning her between the two of them as they all drifted to sleep.

Conner stopped Lilith in the hall before they returned to their rooms.

"How would you like to ruin the Mistress?" he asked quietly

"More than anything as long as I can take that goody goody bitch Grace with her." She said just as quietly

"Why, what do you have against the Mistress?" she asked

"Come with me to my chamber." He said and continued down the hall.

Lilith followed Conner into his chamber watching as he walked over to the bed, reaching under and behind it to wiggle a brick in the wall free revealing a key hidden there. When he stood again, he was unlocking the cage incasing his cock, dropping it onto the bed before licking his palm and taking his stiff shaft in a tight grip stroking hard with a guttural noise in his throat then looked at Lilith with lust in his eyes.

"You going to watch, or would you like to help a guy out?" He raised an eyebrow slowing his strokes waiting for an answer.

"I'll watch and wait as long as you don't go fuzzy and muddled headed like most men after they blow their cock." Lilith found the chair in the room and sat down to wait staring at him as he jerked off shooting a creamy load onto the mattress in front of him.

"Now what did you have in mind?" She asked as he wiped his hand off on the bed.

"I'm going to kill her prized stallion and burn this fucking place to the ground." He said sitting on the floor in front of her and began stroking her ankle.

Lilith laughed and kicked his hand out of the way as she stood up to pace.

"Kill Marcus.... Are you out of your fucking mind?" She turned to stare at him.

"What makes you think you even can? What do you have against him anyway?"

"He's a self-proclaimed holier than thou jack ass, who thinks he's intitled to take whatever he wants without facing the consequences." He unfolded himself as he spoke staking towards her with as evil glint in his eyes. When he reached her, he gripped her hair in a firm grip forcing her head back to take her mouth in a punishing kiss.

When he broke the kiss, he forced Lilith to the bed, bending her torso over the bed and spreading her legs wide.

Lilith reacted purely out of instinct rearing up against his hold, when Conner smacked her ass and jerked her head forcing the side of her face against the bed, Lilith spoke.

"You're not a sub at all are you?" she asked slightly muffled.

"Not in the lest my little bitch, it's all in the end game." With that he thrust his once again hard cock into her wet pussy, fucking her until he jerked then came without waiting to get her off.

He pulled out and pushed her onto the bed climbing in after her, then reached for a cigarette lighting it before speaking again.

"So, what do you have against Grace so bad?" he asked.

"You want to sit here and hash out a plan and talk about revenge after you've blown twice, but not let me cum?" Lilith scoffed.

Conner's hand landed with a loud crack against her pussy before his single sentence reply.

"Yes, now my little whore answer the question."

And so, they talked and planned into the night, fucking when Conner wanted only occasionally letting Lilith cum when he chose.

Bridgett woke the next morning to a hand softly stroking her hip, and when she opened her eyes, Marcus was staring at her with Grace still asleep between them and a patient look in his eyes.

"Are you feeling better love?" He asked softly.

She smiled at him with a quite chuckle. "Yeah, I'm feeling better."

11

Chapter Eleven

Two nights after the Mistress had played with them all so spectacularly Grace found herself summoned to the Mistress's parlor for a private evening of just the two of them. Her knock was answered by one of the younger subs. And after Grace entered the parlor, the Mistress issued a short command.

"Leave us." And the sub left with a slight bow and not a word.

The mistress then rose her flowing dark green gown held in by a black corset slid around her like a cloud, as she walked over to embrace Grace in a hug and lead her to a small table set with a meal for two. When Grace was seated Mistress stroked her hair and shoulders before going around to take her own seat.

"So, my darling girl we need to have a talk about your past." Mistress said frankly as she sipped at her wine.

"And what part of my past are you hoping to learn about Mistress?" Grace asked as she too sipped at a glass of wine.

"Well .... aren't we a blunt little pet tonight?" Mistress stated with a wicked smile.

Grace set her wine down with a sharp thunk as she quickly bowed her head.

"Forgive me Mistress." She said quietly.

"I'm sorry Gracie my pet, it was just an observation is all, but we do need to talk about your last Master." Bridgett said gently, reaching out to stroke the back of her hand.

"What would you like to know about him Mistress?" Grace asked picking up her wine again.

"Why don't you start at the beginning and go from there." Bridgett suggested.

Grace took another sip from her wine before putting it down and folding her hands in her lap.

"I was five years old when my mother was sold to the Master, the training house we were at decided they no longer wanted to put up with an object that had had the bad sense to go and get herself knocked up. So, they found a buyer that was willing to take both of us. Though she had to be willing to let him start training me when I turned fifteen." Grace paused for another sip of wine.

The Mistress just sat there quietly waiting. So, Grace continued.

"I was thirteen when my mom got sick, and I found out about the deal they had made, but less than a year later she was dead, and the Master started my training then." She picked at her meal some before going on when the Mistress still said nothing.

"The Master was never physically cruel to me though he did punish me and use the floggers and paddles on me, fucking me when he saw fit. The only marks he left on me are the nipple rings. But he made me watch everything he did to all the others." Her hands were shaking slightly as she picked up her wine this time.

Mistress reach out and slid her hand over the one Grace still had on the table and gripped it softly.

"How long did this go on?" She asked.

"Five years, then he was killed in a gambling dispute, and I found my way here." Grace said setting her wine aside.

"Grace ... did your mother ever talk about the training house?" Bridgett asked finally.

"Not really, when I did ask all, she said was it was a place that always reminded her of how her parents had thrown her away."

At that Mistress stood up and walked around the table taking Grace's hand she pulled her up and lead her from the room.

"I have something I'd like to show you." The Mistress said this as she led Grace down the hall to the door at the end.

"But first you have to promise me something." Mistress said this as she stopped in front of the door.

"What do I need to promise Mistress?" Grace asked quietly.

"You can't tell anyone what goes on in here tonight. Can you do that Pet?"

Grace thought for a little bit, if the Mistress was trusting her with this, she could give the Mistress her word, after all she already had all of Grace's trust.

"Yes, Mistress. I can do that." She said with her head bowed.

The Mistress stepped closer kissing the top of her head and leaning in to nuzzle at her ear and neck, before turning and opening the door.

Marcus was sitting on the couch reading when they walked in, and upon seeing them he rose putting the book aside as he went to stand in front of the two of them.

"Mistress?" Marcus said this with a raised eyebrow and a questioning tone in his voice.

"It's okay Marcus." Mistress said placing a hand on his bare chest before leaning up to kiss his lips.

"Tonight, we're going to let Grace play a bit, and you get to dominate both of us." With that said she stepped back and headed towards the back room.

Marcus stepped over to Grace, stroked her hair and kissed her temple before speaking.

"Stay here Gracie pet, I'll be back to get you in a moment." And he walked away with a stroke of her face.

Marcus then walked into the back room and shut the door gripping Bridgett's hair in a fierce grip he forced her to look at him.

"Bridgett love, what are you playing at?" He asked softly.

"Nothing really." She said just as softly.

"Then what are we doing here tonight? You never let me dominate you in front of the subs." He asked and stated two incredibly good points.

She sighed and leaned into his hold on her hair.

"You're right Grace is special." She said after a moment.

"But?" He questioned.

"Her mother is dead, and she knows nothing of the training house they were at before their last Master."

That was something to touch on for another night, so for tonight he would keep it simple which seemed to be what Bridgett was after.

"And what are we playing at tonight?" He asked.

"I decided I wanted to let her play with me, guide her through it and let's all have some fun."

"You want to teach Grace how to dominate?" he asked still searching her eyes.

"I want to see what she can do without restrictions on her." Bridgett replied.

"Okay love, then get that fine ass naked, I'll be back with our sub." He kissed her temple and released her to go get Grace.

"Okay Gracie my pet, here's what we're going to do tonight." He said as he came back over to her.

"The Mistress has decided to let you play a little, and see how you do at dominating, but I'm still going to be in charge. Do you understand so far?" He was stroking at her hair as he said this looking into her eyes.

"Yes Master, but..." She trailed off with a slight frown.

"But what pet?" he asked.

"I don't know how to dominate." She said softly looking a little ashamed.

"That's alright pet." He kissed her forehead.

"That's what tonight is about, trust me, and we'll get you to where you need to be."

"But there is a rule in my back room... and that's no clothes." He nipped at her jaw while removing her dress, then lead her to the back room.

When Grace entered the room, she just stopped and stared, it wasn't exactly like anything that she had been expecting. There was a very large bed against one wall, a hip high table in the center of the room, a spanking bench off to the side of it, and one wall held a rack with floggers, paddles, and other toys to play with. And there was the Mistress standing naked near the table with her head bowed waiting like any of the other subs might do. But what was she supposed to do with this? Her first instinct was to go over and kneel before the Mistress, but Marcus had told her that she was the one who would be dominating tonight, and she was as lost as a fish out of water would be.

Marcus walked up behind Grace and wrapped his arms around her middle bringing her back against his now naked body nuzzling at her neck before speaking.

"What do you want to do to her Gracie love?" He asked in a husky voice.

"I don't know." Grace replied quietly tilting her head back against his shoulder.

"Then look at her and tell me what you see." He said with his lips on her temple.

Grace picked her head up off his shoulder and looked at the Mistress, with her head bowed the tendrils she had left out of her up do where hanging down to block some of the view of her face, but that wasn't the most noticeable. Her tanned skin had a flushed glow to it, and her nipples were tight dusky brown peeks sticking out waiting for attention, as Grace continued her scan down the Mistress's body, she found her legs slightly spread and she could just see the glistening of moisture on the inside of her parted thighs, and Grace licked her lips on a soft sigh at the sight.

"What do you see Gracie." Marcus asked again

"I see need, and desire. I see submission and want." She said as she kept her gaze fixed in the junction between the Mistress's thighs.

"And what would you do about that?" Marcus asked.

"I would make her feel, let her cum." Grace said tentatively.

"Show me how you would do this." Marcus said beginning to walk her over to the Mistress. Almost creating a dance of their own.

When they were standing within inches of the Mistress Grace hesitantly reached up her hand and brushed the side of her face before sliding her hand down along the side of her neck to her shoulder, but when the Mistress lifted her head and looked at Grace she froze and jerked her hand away suddenly.

"Gracie love, remember you're in charge tonight." Marcus growled nipping at her neck in reprimand.

Grace turned her head towards him with a question. "Can I blindfold her?"

"You're in charge." He said again.

"If you want to blindfold her, then do it."

"Where are they?" She asked stepping out of his arms.

"There's a set of drawers over by the bed." He said letting her go with a rub to her hip.

Marcus watched Grace walk over to the bed and begin to look through the set of drawers there, before looking back to Bridget. She still had her head up and was looking back at him, he could see the need and desire that Grace had spoken of in her eyes, and the slight movements she was making, a gentle sway to her body, the small panting of her breath, her nipples were hardening even more and he imagined they were becoming a little painful without something there to tease them, and then there was the opaque haze forming in her emerald eyes.

Grace opened the first drawer and stared for a minute, inside she found a variety of different kinds of lubes and oils, nipple clamps and chains and weights to go with them, there were also several pairs of handcuffs from steel to soft leather. But she didn't see any blindfolds, so she shut that drawer and opened the one under it. And that's where she found the blindfolds along with several lengths of silk rope and strands of creamy white pearls. She knew how the pearls felt sliding along her skin, the Mistress enjoyed teasing her with their coolness before sliding them through her hot sensitive folds She wondered how the Mistress would reacted to feeling them on her, Grace picked up one of the strands letting it slid through her fingers like water before winding them around her hand, reaching down again she selected a blood red silk blindfold before shutting the drawer to head back to where Marcus and the Mistress were waiting.

When she got back to them Grace approached the Mistress from behind tentatively sliding the hand with the pearls wrapped around it up Mistress's back smiling when she heard the mistress sigh and arch her back a little. When Grace got to her neck, she gripped it slightly and kneaded for a minute at the tight muscles she found there before releasing her to uncoil the pearls and drape them over the Mistress's shoulder to hang seductively between her breasts. She then gathered the blindfold in both her hands and reached up to secure it around the Mistress's eyes tying it snuggly at the back of her head. When Grace can back around to the front, she shyly stroked a hand down the center of Marcus's chest before leaning up to kiss him lightly.

Marcus kissed Grace back before removing her hand and turning her to face the Bridget.

"Focus on her Gracie." He said with a little swat to her hip.

"Now that she's blind what do you want to do?"

Grace didn't answer, instead she freed her arm from his light grip and stepped closer to the Mistress placing her hands on her hips before gliding them up to cupped and squeeze the underside of her breast leaning forward, she lightly licked one of the Mistress's tight nipples flicking and kissing it before moving to repeat the same moves on the other nipple.

When the Mistress reached up to grip Grace's hair to hold her in place wanting more contact, Marcus moved behind her to secure her hands at her back, so Grace had free rein to do what she pleased whispering in her ear when he was behind her.

"It feels good doesn't it darling?"

When she whimpered, he laughed against her ear?

"She' so tentative it will slowly drive you mad." He bit her ear hard causing her to gasp and jerk against his hold on her. And Marcus saw Grace drop her hold on Bridgett.

Marcus released Bridgett's ear and spoke with steel in his voice.

"Gracie don't stop what you're doing."

"Master?" she replied softly.

"She's going to move love, it's just her body's reaction to what you do, you felt her shiver at your contact yes?"

"Yes, I did."

"Her jerk came from me biting her ear lobe." He said licking at the Mistress's neck.

Grace smiled a little before sliding her arms around the Mistress's waist brushing at Marcus's hips before taking the Mistress's mouth it a hungry kiss stroking her back up then down to grip her ass, spreading her cheeks so Marcus's cock could slide between them when she moved her lips across Bridgett's chin to her ear licking where Marcus had bit before working her way down to her throat, and back up again to whisper in Mistress's ear.

"Do you like the feel of that?" she asked tentatively as she moved her hands from Bridgett's ass to her hip and then up the middle of her body to curl the pearls around her middle and ring fingers before sliding them over her body to tease at her tight nipples.

Bridgett moaned and turned her head into Grace's neck to nuzzle there, then heard Marcus laugh softly against her neck.

"Words loves." He said nipping at the opposite side from where Grace was still at.

"More." She breathed against Grace's neck.

Marcus released one of her arms and smacked her ass with a loud crack, causing her to yelp and bit down on Grace's neck, the effect had her ass squeezing around his stiff shaft.

"More what?" Marcus demanded.

"Master please." She said quickly

"Love I'm not the one asking or leading right now." He smacked her ass again.

"Mistress More .... Please." Bridgett nuzzled at Grace's neck again before bowing her forehead against her shoulder.

"Good girl." Marcus whispered kissing the back of Bridgett's neck while taking ahold of her free arm again.

Grace lifted her head from where she was kissing and nuzzling at the Mistress's neck and smiled at Marcus over her shoulder as she slid her pearl circled fingers lower to work them gently through her wet folds. Her smile growing even bigger when the Mistress moaned and bit at her shoulder again.

Grace was slowly driving her mad; Bridgett couldn't seem to get her bearings with Grace dominating her from the front and Marcus restraining her from behind, and his cock at her ass she was surrounded by feeling. The solid wall of Marcus and the soft curves of Grace she wanted it to stop and never end at the same time.

Grace slowly worked her pearl clad fingers into the Mistress's core pumping in a few inches then stopping and letting her absorb the feeling before pushing a little farther in. When she had worked her fingers in as far as she could she stopped and breathed against the Mistress's neck before biting it hard and fucking her fast and hard enjoying the feeling of her clenching muscles as she started to cum jerking and straining against her and Marcus, biting at Grace as hard as she was biting at her.

Marcus groaned into Bridgett's hair as he felt her ass squeeze around his cock causing it to stiffen even more than it already was and when he felt her cum as Grace fucked her with pearl wrapped fingers, he let go shooting his cum onto Bridgett's back as well as his stomach, breathing heavily into her hair as he regained some of his senses.

When Grace felt Mistress start to calm, she slowly pulled her fingers free wincing as the Mistress winced knowing the sensations she was feeling. With her fingers free she dropped the pearls to the floor to reach up and trace the Mistress's parted lips with her pussy flavored fingers before moving them over to Marcus's lips and thrusting them in as she kissed the Mistress thrusting her tongue deep with a hungry noise.

"Lay her out on the table." Grace said to Marcus when she broke the kiss and pulled her fingers free from his mouth.

Marcus took three steps forward propelling both women with him, and when he had Bridgett just past the edge of the table, he pushed her releasing her arms to lay her out like a pagan offering, moving to the head of the table. Guiding her arms up so he could secure them with rope around the hook at the top.

Meanwhile Grace stroked her body teasing and continuing to arouse as she went. When she reached up and pinched Bridgett's nipples suckling one into her mouth to tease with her teeth and tongue, Bridgett arched her back with a throaty moan and moved her legs, so they could circle Grace's flared hips to pull her closer, seeking any form of friction to ease the aching need in her core.

In moments Marcus was behind Grace prying the Mistress's thighs apart.

"None of that now love." He tisked.

"Let Grace have her fun."

And he went about securing her thighs, so she was wide open, then came back behind Grace stroking her spine before smacking her ass soundly causing her to bite down hard on the nipple her was playing with, with a loud groan, getting a jerk of the body and a cry from the Mistress in return.

Grace lifted her head and gave Marcus an impish look.

"I thought I was in charge tonight?" she said with a pout.

"You are pet, I just enjoying spanking your fine ass." Marcus replied gripping her hair to pull her in for a kiss of his own, enjoying Bridgett's flavor on Grace's lips and tongue before letting her return to her play.

Grace went back to her task at hand squeezing Bridgett's tits before licking, nipping, and kissing her way south, pausing at the Mistress's naval to circle her tongue teasing and tormenting before moving down to tentatively lick at the Mistress's dripping wet folds.

Bridgett whimpered and moaned between gasps and little cries as she absorbed what Grace was doing to her. The girl may not be experienced in dominating, but when given a free leash she certainly knew how to play with a body. Her shy little touches, hesitant kisses, and licks were enough to send a weaker person over the edge a dozen times or more. Then the first little flick of that seeking tongue as it hit Bridgett's clit had her fighting against her bonds, moaning and trying to thrust up for more pressure.

Marcus watched as Bridgett fought for control, the tremors of her body visible as he idly ran his hand up and down Grace's back, when he reached her hair again, he took it in his fist pulling Grace back just enough so he could work his fingers in-between her mouth and Bridgett's clit rubbing and pinching at it as Grace continued to lick and suck. And when he saw Bridgett start to fall his moved his fingers down and fucked them into her tight hot core with a command to Grace to suck that clit hard. Bridgett's screams echoed off the walls as she came hard clamping down on his fingers like a vise.

Marcus watched Bridgett come back down as he gently slid his fingers free, moving them over to Grace's pussy to play with her. Pulling on her hair to bring her back to his chest he worked her folds getting her wetter and wetter smiling against her throat as he listened to her start to whimper.

"Kneel on the table pet, get this burning pussy as close to hers as possible I want to be able to play with you both." He bit at her throat as she Shakely climbed onto the table, while he continued to play with her.

Marcus shifted the hand he had in her hair to circle her throat, all the while rubbing and stroking at her folds feeling Bridgett's quivering muscles as he worked Grace into a slow shaky fall of an orgasm that had her moaning and gripping at his arms searching for a hold, and the little jerks of her hips causing his knuckles to rub at Bridgett's sensitive folds making her fall again with a mewling whimper.

When Grace relaxed her hands and started to come down Marcus bent her torso over Bridgett, locking Grace's wrists on the same hook that left her mouth right in the crook of Bridgett's neck before breaking all contact to walk over to a table where he had several different oils and an assortment of different sizes of anal plugs, dildos, and pearls. Choosing two large plugs, a medium strand of pearls, a large glass cock, and the bottle of warming oil Marcus went back to the table sliding the pearls across Grace's back as he sat the toys and the oil on the table near Bridgett's hip.

Leaning over the two of them he spoke.

"How are my girls doing?" and he laughed when all he got in response were whimpers and moans.

Grace slowly lifted her head to look at him over her shoulder with sleepy eyes.

"You took over control." She pouted with a mischievous look in her eyes.

"Oh, you impish little pet...you may get to play, but I'm always in control in my room." Marcus gripped her hair keeping her teeth away from Bridgett's soft neck then brought his pearls wrapped hand down on Grace's ass in a hard smack causing her to scream out and close her eyes absorbing the sensation.

Marcus spanked Grace five more times before leaning over her and biting down on her shoulder hard enough to leave a deep purple mark that he licked at too sooth after he pulled away.

"I'm a greedy old bastard Gracie pet." He breathed against the nap of her neck, before standing up again.

"It's time for me to take over and play with the both of you." He spanked her ass again before rubbing the pearls over Bridgett's dripping fold getting her to thrash against her bonds only to rub against the pearls and Grace at the same time causing her to gasp at the feelings.

Pulling his hands away from the girls Marcus picked up the oil and spilled a good amount between Grace's lovely red cheeks rubbing it around and into her tight back hole fucking her ass slowly with his thumb before reaching for one of the plugs and working it into her body watching as it nestled nice and snug showing only the deep purple jewel against her pale flesh then he smacked her ass again as he picked up the pearls and worked them into her clenching pussy inch by inch until five inches were rolling teasingly against her inner walls every time she squeezed her muscles together trying to find some relief.

"You enjoy the torture don't you pet?" Marcus asked as he soothed her with small circles on her lower back.

Grace heard Marcus's voice as if it was far away in a fog and she could only moan in response.

Marcus laughed as he changed his hand to rake his blunt nails down her back leaving red welts before he smacked her ass again causing Grace to scream and bit down on Bridgett's throat.

When he finished working Grace's ass over he moved on to priming Bridgett's ass for the large plug, smiling at her throaty moan as he rubbed the warm oil over her open crack, stilling when she started moving her hips seeking more , then reached for the plug working it into her tight hole until all he saw was a green jewel, as he stroked at her inner thighs and mound he picked up the glass dildo to work it slowly into Grace's pearl filled pussy smiling as her body quivered from the sensations.

With Grace panting quietly as the glass cock settled into her tight core Marcus took ahold of his cock teasing it along Bridgett's wet folds before thrusting fast and hard into her tight core then paused as Bridgett jerked hard enough to move the table several inches as she calmed some he began a slow and hard steady pace, he knew that the toys inside Grace moved each time he thrust into Bridgett and he could feel Grace squirming trying to find some kind of relief. As he felt Bridgett tighten around him and start to shake, he slid a hand between the two hot pussies working their sensitive clits until they were both whimpering and moaning through orgasms only then did, he let himself go jerking and shooting his creamy load into Bridgett's gripping core.

When Marcus calmed a bit, he slowly pulled free of Bridgett soothing her and Grace as he removed the toys from the both of them. Releasing both women's wrists then carried Grace to the bed covering her still shaking body before going back and gathered Bridgett into his arm nuzzling at her neck as he walked back to the bed slipping the both of them under the covers draping an arm over Bridgett to rest his hand on Grace's tummy as they all drafted off to sleep.

_12_

Chapter Twelve

Conner sat at the desk in his room with paper and pen in front of him forgotten as he stared at the picture in his hand stroking his thumb over and over the cheek and lips of the woman that was in it, how many years had it been? Seven or ten, why couldn't he remember. He wished he could still remember the feel of her silky soft skin and the flow of her hair as he gripped it in his hand, why was the red he saw in his mind the blood that had coated her creamy skin instead of the redness of his handprint on her lovely ass.

"who is she?" Lilith asked.

Conner started and slipped the picture back into a hidden drawer on his desk quickly before turning to face the sub on his bed. he hadn't heard Lilith stir, and it went to show how far gone he really was.

"Just someone from my past, and no one for you to be concerned with my little whore."

He rose from the chair going over to the wardrobe to pull out several lengths of rope, a ball gag, a wooden paddle, and a large steel anal plug. Walking back to the bed he issued a command for Lilith to kneel on the bed with her back to him. Watching her obey he sat all but two lengths of rope and the ball gag on the side table near the bed when he turned to her he fit the gag in her mouth securing it behind her head before wrapping a portion of the rope around her hair forcing her head back in a sharp angle as he then wrapped it around her forearms after he placed them together so they were parallel with the bed, from there he doubled the other rope looping it around her arms before running it into her ass crack and pussy folds then up to tie it around her throat.

Stepping back, he picked up a cane that he always kept by his bed snapping it across her ass without warning or warm up leaving deep red welts on her flesh smiling as she screamed. Finished with that he turned her head forcing it down to the mattress using the last of the rope to secure her thighs open exposing her wet folds to whatever he wanted to do to them. He stroked them for a bit rolling the rope back and forth heightening the feeling as he worked her moisture up and into her ass until he could fuck the plug nice and deep, before he set to work paddling her ass with a wooden paddle that had about a dozen holes in it swinging it harder and harder every time she screamed, when her screams turned into whimpers he dropped the paddle and fucked her pussy fast and hard until he came with a grunt pulling out before Lilith could come, only to collapse into his chair and watch her shake as he finished his drink.

Lilith laid there with her tears soaking the bed around her trying to make sense out of everything. There were dozens of sensations flowing through her the sharp angle of her head had pain shooting through her every time she tried to move slightly, and her arms were starting to ache from being so far behind her, but it was the ropes between her pussy lips she felt the most. They rolled side to side with just the slightest movements that had her shaking and tensing wondering if she would finally fall ending the longing for more. And it all made her wonder if she had found and sided with someone even worse than her last Master.

Conner saw Lilith start to relax into her bonds as her shaking stopped, and he decided that he couldn't have that, so he rose taking his glass with him he pulled three ice cubes out and fucked them into her hot core causing her to thrush and scream.

He laughed; the sadistic bastard laughed as he finger fucked the ice into her pussy. Was he going to let her come this time or was he just playing another game? Lilith withered against her bonds trying so hard to find something.... anything. she whimpered and moaned feeling the cold of the ice and the rough of the rope. Trying to beg around the gag. When his hand moved, she whimpered again trying to fallow it, and then the paddle came again over and over till she couldn't feel her ass anymore. When it stopped, she sighed into the bed then felt the world tilt and she was thrown onto her back, open and exposed her head still at that sharp angle and her arms so far behind her it thrust her tits up and out, Conner pinched and play with her nipples before bending over to suck and bite at them all the while rubbing his cock against her sensitive clit. When she started to try and move her hips to get a firmer pressure he laughed and leaned up to bite her throat hard before pulling back to bring the paddle down on her wet folds drawing a shriek from around the gag.

"I'm in charge whore." Two smacks of the paddle.

"I get to tell you when to move or cum." Three smacks of the paddle.

Lilith screamed again and again trying to get away, but she couldn't move. When the paddle stopped, she breathed a sigh of relief, then felt him thrust into her fucking her until she was on the edge before pulling out and fisting his cock till, he came on her stomach, his warm sticky cum sliding over her abdomen. She listened to him breathing heavily as he walked away then she heard the shower coming on in the bathroom.

Lilith lay still tied up on the bed quaking with need as her mind wandered. Was her revenge really worth this, at least her old Master had let her cum instead of leaving her hanging on this edge, and this was the second time she had found herself in this situation since arriving here. But Grace still needed to be punished in Lilith's eyes, so she shifted slightly trying to find a more comfortable positions while she waited for Conner to come out of the bathroom and release her.

As Conner came out of the bathroom, he picked a knife up from the cabinet where the toys were stored returning to the bed to cut the ropes from Lilith's body but not before sliding the flat side of the blade over her heated skin causing goose bumps to rise on her flesh.

"Now whore I want you to stay open for me as we talk." He said as he let her legs relax down to the bed while leaving them spread, but he kept her arms bound behind her.

Lilith mumbled something around the gag and looked at him with angry eyes.

Conner smack her pussy once in reprimand before reaching up to remove the gag.

"You know if you weren't such an obstinate little whore your master's probably wouldn't treat you this way." He remarked as he pulled the gag away from her mouth.

"Well, if you would actually let me cum, I might not act this way so much." She said when her mouth was free.

Conner reacted like lighting striking, gripping her throat tight enough to cut off her air. "I told you whore I'm in charge and I tell you when to cum, you haven't errand it yet."

He released her and stood pacing the room like a caged animal.

"There's an auction coming up in a few days." Conner stated

"Are you on the block?" He asked continuing his pacing without even looking at her.

"No, the Mistress is afraid I'll run my mouth off to a client." Lilith sneered.

"She's probably right." Conner laughed stopping to smack her pussy when she looked at him with loathing in her eyes.

"It's probably good anyway, it means that you don't have to try and explain the marks on your body." Toying with her clit some before walking away.

"Unfortunately, I am on the block, I'll have some prissy little Female Dom want a be telling me how to worship her all night." It was his turn to sneer.

"And what's wrong with that?" Lilith remarked.

"At least she'll let you cum multiple times throughout the night."

"Are you saying you want to cum my little whore?" Conner raised his eyebrow at her almost daring her to say something.

"What do you think?" She asked looking at him with a burning need in her eyes.

"Well, aren't we in a mood." Conner stopped at the cabinet and pulled a crop out before walking back to the bed to re-secure her legs keeping them open for his assault.

With that done he stepped back and brought the crop down directly on her swollen clit once, twice getting gasps and moans from her lips, but the third time he brought it down with more force she screamed and thrashed against her bonds shaking and shuttering, and he didn't stop there he dropped the crop and fucked his fingers into her tight pulsing pussy fucking her over and over never letting her come down from the high. When his fingers started to cramp, he pulled them out replacing them with his mouth licking, sucking, and biting at her as she whimpered and begged incoherently. Having enough of that he rose and picked up a glass cock starting with a fast thrust getting another scream from her lips.

"You said you wanted to cum whore, I'm just being an indulgent Master." Conner explained as he fucked the glass shaft into her faster and faster.

Lilith whimpered and gasped feeling everything and nothing all at once. She came over and over her body slowly going numb, but never had enough time to enjoy the heady rush before he took her up and over again. Finally, he pulled the hard glass cock from her burning pussy only to fuck his hard-throbbing cock into her and fucking her into a screamingly intense orgasm that had her blacking out from the intensity.

Conner watched his whore cum over and over, her skin flushed and quivering with need and exhaustion, and when he thrust his hard cock into her taking her over that final edge watching her black out and go lacks, he continued to fuck her gripping pussy until he found his own release then collapsed back into the chair at his desk.

Well, that didn't go quite like he had planned. The bitch just didn't know when to stop challenging every little thing, and he was beginning to think she was more trouble than he needed. Whores were supposed to do as they were told, shut their mouths, and get on their backs or their knees and take what their owners deemed to give them.

Staring at the unconscious woman on his bed he blindly searched his desk behind him coming up with a bottle of the Mistress's prized scotch. Taking a swig directly from the bottle he started to reformulate his plan and adjust his timetable. Thinking he had just enough time to do a little clean up and still execute his plan a little ahead of schedule. So, he stared and planned in his head as he finished half the bottle before standing to cut the ropes from Lilith and wrap her in a blanket to heft her over his shoulder and sneak out of the manor.

Lilith came awake slowly, her arms aching and straining in a different way than they were earlier as they were now secured above her head leaving her suspended inches off the ground. As the fogginess cleared from her head, she lifted it and looked around it was different a room then they had been in before, where were they. She couldn't remember anything, what happened?

"Awe so the whore is finally awake." Conner said from somewhere behind her.

"Don't try to remember anything, it's just going to make your head hurt, you woke up halfway here and I had to give you a little something to knock you out again. You wouldn't be remembering anything of the last twelve hours or so. Not that it's really going to matter." He stroked her as he said this close to her ear.

"See I've decided that I don't really need you to execute my plan, so we're going to have to say goodbye." He walked away to get something.

"Then why do you have me tired up like you still plan to use me?" Lilith commented trying to turn her head to see where he was at.

"Let me tell you a little something about this cabin whore. See I found this a while ago and decided that it would work for my little side hobby." He had come back up behind her and looped a ball gag over her head to fit in her mouth before turning her so she could see what was displayed on the mantle.

Lilith's eyes bugled and she started to cough as she choked on the saliva in her mouth when she inhaled sharply. Lined up neatly on the mantle where 6 human skulls each had a piece of jewelry laid out in front of it, and a picture of a woman hanging from the wall above it.

"You see my little whore, I like to bring pretty little whores just like you here, you know the curious ones that want to know more or like to play on the wild side, and I play with them. Showing them all the way, they can receive pain and pleasure as I fuck them. Most of them sweet little virgins getting their first taste of a cock before I start slicing at their silky soft skin with cold steel. And they feel so... good as I fuck them while I slit their throats. But that's a story for another time, now it's time to play with me disobedient little whore." He walked around her stroking her skin with feather light touches getting goose bumps to rise.

Lilith shivered as he continued to play with her, flinching as he squeezed her tits together hard marveling slightly as her nipples hardened when he released her tits to circle them with light touches. When he flicked her rings, she moaned around the gag, and then shrieked as he ripped them from her body.

Conner leaned into her and licked the blood from her skin as she hung there shaking from the pain and need. He circled the other hole gathering her blood on his fingers before taking them down to fuck them into her pussy that clinched around them, and when he circled his thumb on her clit, she came hard.

Conner lifted his head pulling free of her body, walking over to a table to pick up a small dagger before circling her he started making little cuts into the scars on her back drawing small designs at his whim. When he got down to her ass, he carved a dozen or so tiny hearts into each cheek then smacking them over and over smiling as she screamed around the gag.

Satisfied with her back he circled around to her front. Starting at the hallow of her throat he ran the dagger down leaving a shallow cut all the way down to the top of her shaved mound. Watching the tears gather and seep from her eyes he made little exes across her quivering abdomen working up to her bleeding breasts taking the tip around one at a time carving circle into them.

Dropping the dagger, he procced to lick and kiss the blood from her body, Lilith was quaking and whimpering around the gag trying to figure out what was going on or what she had done so wrong. But the big thing she couldn't figure out was why she was so turned on and wanting him to fuck her so desperately. When he reached her throat kissing and licking then biting down on the tender flesh there she moaned as he fucked his thick cock into her hot pulsing core fucking her hard and fast letting her come screaming against the gag before he found his release.

Pulling out of her he walked behind her to pick up a barbed metal flogger and working her back and ass with hard brutal strokes a dozen hits or so before lubing his cock with her blood. Gripping her hair in a tight hold and fucking her ass until he came again. He repeated this over and over going to her front and then to her back staying with the metal flogger liking the marks it made on her golden skin. Seeing her hanging there close to passing out Conner changed the flogger for the dagger, fucking into her pussy. Placing the dagger at her throat he fucked her hard, and when she was about come, he slit her throat finding his release as the life went out of her abused body.

Conner pulled out of her lifeless body and still bloody from the torture went about gathering up his treasures storing them and his newly acquired nipple rings in a bag before he went to clean himself up, and as he left the cabin with his bag in hand, he dosed the cabin in liquor then set a match to it as he headed back to the manor.

13

Chapter Thirteen

In the wee hours of the morning Marcus stood in the shadows and watched Conner slip back into the manor. Furrowing his brow, he stepped from the shadows.

"Where the hell have you been all night sub?" He asked causing Conner to start before he turned to face Marcus.

"None of your business lapdog." Conner sneered and went to continue to his chamber.

Marcus grabbed Conner's arm and forced him to face him.

"I'm no lapdog, and you damn well know it. If I question you about where you've been going at night against the rules you answer the fucking question." Marcus stared at Conner waiting with his hand like iron wrapped around the man's forearm.

Conner jerked his arm trying to get free of Marcus, but the man had a steel like grip on him. So, he lied.

"I couldn't sleep, so I went for a walk. Now let me go lapdog." But he couldn't quite get rid of the sneer.

Marcus held on for a bit longer before releasing him with a warning.

"Watch it sub you're on thin ice with both me and the Mistress." And he walked away.

Conner watched as Marcus left the front hall heading to the back of the manor. He couldn't believe that man thinking he wasn't a lapdog for the bitch of a Mistress, he must say she trained the dick well. Conner shook his head and went to find his bed; killing really took the energy out of a man. Though he would have beautiful dreams this morning as he recalled the sounds of Lilith's screams as he carved up her luscious body.

Marcus returned to his chamber to find Bridgett sitting on the couch gloriously naked holding a cup of tea.

"And where did you run off to this morning love?" She asked before taking a slow sip.

"Conner's been sneaking out of the manor; I wanted to see if he had done it last night and to talk to him about it." Marcus said collapsing onto the couch next to her.

"Really, and how have I not noticed this." Bridgett commented.

"Because you've been wrapped up in dealing with Grace and Lilith, love." Marcus laughed.

"Oh right. So, did you get any answers this morning?"

"No, all I got was snide remarks and comments, and something about going for a walk because he couldn't sleep." Marcus sighed as he leaned his head back against the couch.

"There's something about him that picks at the back of my mind." He continued with his eyes closed.

"He looks at me like I've done something to him, but I don't know."

"Well have you asked him about it." Bridgett nudged his thigh with her foot.

Marcus quirked his lip slightly and grabbed her ankle to bring her foot onto his lap to start stroking her calf with light rhythmic caresses.

"I don't think it would be that simple." He said

"You see I didn't take the time we were apart really well love, and I spent most of that time at the bottom of a bottle. It could be that I maybe took a lover that was his, and even more than three sheets to the wind I can still charm a lady into my bed and out of her clothes faster than most." He cracked an eye open to peek at her.

"I'll agree that you're a charmer alright." She laughed

"But what makes you think you stole a lover from him?"

"The way he looks at me when he thinks I don't see him. Then there's the picture I found in his room when I searched it one night. It's a woman I remember, she was a pretty red headed sub that obeyed all my drunken commands with an eagerness I hadn't seen in a long time, but in my haze, I didn't realize she already had a Master, and when he confronted us one night, she was killed in the fall out." He set her foot back on the couch and rose to pace.

"Where is Grace." He asked

"She's still asleep in the back room." Bridgett said rising to stand next to him.

"Marcus what happened?" She rubbed at his back as he stared at nothing.

"I was killed too love, and this cruse brought me back next to a bloody ravished body I barely recognized, what was done to her in a rage..." His whole body shuttered.

"I'm so sorry Marcus, when was this?" she placed a soft kiss on his shoulder blade still rubbing his back in soothing strokes.

"It happened just before I came and found you again; I sobered up after that night, and then went to get you." He turned around and wrapped his arms around her warm body.

"I know it's hard love, but we'll get through this." She rested her head on his chest wrapping her arms around his back.

"Come back to bed." She whispered after a bit.

Marcus sighed, kissed her hair, and lead them both back to the backroom where they curled around a sleeping Grace and fell back to sleep.

As Marcus slipped back into sleep the dream hit him like a sledge-hammer.

He walked into his top floor penthouse to a glass shattering scream, and he ran to his playroom stumbling drunkenly against the walls as he went. Opening the door, he found his latest sub hanging from a hook in the ceiling with blood seeping from dozens of shallow wounds and smeared over her shaking body. Another scream ripped from her lips, and he shifted to see the man standing behind her with a barbed flogger.

"This is what happens when my subs try and leave before I'm done with them." The man said striking her again.

"Awe so your savior has arrived." He smiled viciously with her blood coating his skin.

The man moved like a flash striking Marcus unconscious. When he woke, he was tied to a chair, and the sub was crying as he heard her being fucked roughly, and he screamed around the gag in his mouth as he watched the man slit the subs throat before coming at him and slitting his throat.

Marcus awoke with his heart pounding. Getting up quietly he left the girls sleeping and went to get a drink. Where had that come from? He shakily downed two fingers of scotch then went to take a long hot shower.

14

Chapter Fourteen

The night of the auction the whole manor was abuzz with activity, those that were on the block for the night were in the back of the auction hall getting ready, The Mistress there inspecting them to make sure they were at their finest, naked with a supple black leather collar and matching leash around their throats. And those that weren't on the block wandered among the guests with trays of drinks and orduvres, also naked but for collars that showed the color of their training level.

All the while Grace and Marcus sat on a raised dais draped in the wine-red silk of their station, on display but not for sale. The settee they lounged on was arranged next to a throne like chair that placed Marcus head just above the armrest and Grace laying with her head in his lap it gave the Mistress freedom to stroke her prized pets as she desired.

When the lights flickered the guest went to take their seats and the subs faded into the background, and as the lights dimmed to give the best view of the stage where the merchandise would be presented the Mistress came out from behind the curtain.

"Good evening guests, and welcome to tonight's auction. I can assure you that we have some very prime specimens on the block for you this evening. Though I must remind you to keep things civil and no disrespecting the winning bidder, and with that I turn it over to the auctioneer wishing you all the best of luck." Bridgett exited the stage taking her place on the throne petting both Marcus and Grace as the auction began.

There were ten subs up for bid this night five females and five males. The first on the block was a young female that had begun her training just six months ago and was fast becoming a crowd favorite, and the bidding began at five thousand dollars, going up until finally coming to an end at twenty thousand dollars to an older gentleman that had been coming to the auctions since they started.

The next was a male sub that went to a long-time female guest for fifteen thousand and on it went until coming to the last subs of the night which happened to be Conner this night. When he was led onto the stage his toned tanned body on glorious display with his cock standing proudly at attention. The women in the crowd ohhed in delight, and the bidding began at twenty thousand dollars.

"Well, I'll give him that, he does get the women's panties in a twist." Bridgett remarked as the bidding increased above forty thousand, finally ending at sixty thousand dollars.

Conner kept his head down and a passive look on his face as the woman who paid sixty thousand dollars for him petted, pawed, and pinched at his body as she picked up the leash and leads him from the room like some prized stallion. God these auctions were getting tedious, did these women really think they could control him, and the Mistress making an obscenely large profit out of it, and did the subs see any of it...no. She kept it for herself and lorded it over all but her prized pets. Well, that was going to change, and soon. He would show them.

When the woman had him in her chamber, she slapped him across the face and ordered him to kneel binding his wrist with steel shackles then chaining them to the floor before picking up the flogger and working his back over with giddy delight, giggling with a shrill tone that pieced his skull like needles every time he grunted from the impact. When she tired of flogging him, she ordered him to roll over and slide down so his arms were stretched above his head and she mounted him like a sex starved wild cat, scratching at his chest as she fucked him fast and hard, and when she found her climax, she slapped him again before leaning down to bite his throat.

The fake dominatrix climbed off him and crawled into the bed leaving him there as she fell asleep, the little whore. He heaved an angry sigh and shifted trying to find a way to get comfortable and wait for the whore to wake up and use him again. When she woke again, she knelt on the floor and sucked his still hard cock into her mouth and worked him like he was the last ice cream cone on a hot summer day, and when he blew his load into her greedy mouth, he wanted to wrap his hands around her scrawny neck and squeeze.

And so, the night went on, she was either beating him, fucking him, or blowing his cock. But on the final time she forgot to bind his wrists, and so it was his time to act.

15

Chapter Fifteen

After all guests that had not won had left for the night Bridgett climbed the stairs checking on all the subs that had not been bid on, when she reached Lilith's chamber and found it empty, she frowned think back and realizing that she hadn't seen the girl all night. Starting to get a little irritated she finished checking on the subs and went to find Grace and Marcus.

She found them both in Marcus's chamber on the couch, Marcus was sitting there with Grace's head in his lap like at the auction, only he was stroking her hair this time as she dozed a bit.

"Everything okay love?" Marcus asked when he saw her irritated look. Grace opened her eyes and lifted her head slightly to look at the Mistress.

"Gracie pet would you go into the playroom and wait for us to join you." Bridgett said quietly.

As Grace rose and headed into the playroom without a word Marcus fallowed her up but veered over to Bridgett and when he heard the door close quietly behind Grace he spoke.

"What's going on love? Did something happen as the guests left?"

"Nothing happened with the guest, but when I went to check on the subs Lilith wasn't in her chamber, and I don't remember seeing her during the auction at all." She explained as she stared at his chest stroking it absent mindedly.

Marcus furrowed his brow thinking trying to remember if he had seen her tonight.

"You know that's odd I don't remember seeing her tonight either. But that's a puzzle for tomorrow." He said reaching up to start undressing her.

"Come love lets go play with our pet." He kissed her forehead and lead her now naked body into the playroom.

When they entered the room, they saw that Grace had laid herself over the spanking bench waiting patiently for whatever they would do to her. Upon seeing her Bridgett walked away from Marcus coming up behind Grace to run her hands over her ass and up her pale back raking her fingernails back down before spanking her five times. When she pulled back for a sixth Marcs caught her wrist and gave her ass a smack of its own.

"Come now love you know you need to strap her down before you can start playing with her." He licked her neck and smacked her ass again to get her moving, and he went to pull the table over by Grace's head to put his plan into motion.

When he had the table positioned just right at Grace's head, he stroked her cheek and looked to see if Bridgett had finished stripping her down.

"Come here love." He held out his hand for her inviting her to the table when he saw that she had finished.

Pulling her in for a long deep kiss before laying her out on the table, he stretched her arms above her head and tied a silk rope around her wrists before looping them over a hook at the tabletop. He then looped a rope around her thighs bring them up and out leaving her nice and wide for Grace's mouth, but the angle wasn't quite right. He walked over to the bed grabbing a couple of pillows to slid under her hips bring her wet pussy just close enough for Grace to lick in a light teasing manner. He rubbed his finger through Bridgett's folds teasing her now with firm sure strokes getting desperate little gasps from her lips, when he had coated his fingers in her juicy goodness, he lifted them to Grace's waiting lips tracing them slowly before slipping them into her mouth for her to clean them off then leaning down to take her mouth in a deep brutal kiss and whispering in her ear.

"I'm going to making you scream Gracie pet, and the louder you are the faster she'll cum." He ran his hand down her back as he walked to her beautiful red ass, gripping it before giving it five smacks of his own getting only moans in response.

"We're going to have to do better than that pet." He said reaching over to get a studded paddle off the wall.

He started at the middle of her milky thighs with light little taps over and over getting moans and pants from her that caused Bridgett to start whimpering and moaning. Moving up to the part of her thighs just below her ass he increased the force just a bit getting little cries from her that were getting Bridgett to move trying to get closer to Grace's lips for more.

Before moving up to her ass Marcus stopped to get a couple plugs and some lube, going down to Bridgett he fucked the plug through her folds only to take it up to fuck it into Grace's mouth.

"Keep it there pet." He teased picking up the lube to squirt a good amount onto Bridgett's waiting asshole greasing it up nice and good before popping the plug out of Grace's mouth slowly working it into Bridgett's waiting ass.

"Lick her pussy pet, nice light flicks on that pretty clit." He then moved down to Grace's waiting ass applying a squirt of lube before working his fingers in and out, so he fucked the plug nice and deep in one thrust. With it settled in he took a moment to admire the sparkling jewel, then taking the studded paddle up again he worked her ass over and over getting pretty screams from her lips that got Bridgett crying out begging for more.

Dropping the paddle, he took Grace's hair in a tight grip forcing her face closer to Bridgett's pulsing pussy before he fucked his hard cock into Grace's tight hot core to fuck her hard and fast keeping her screaming against Bridgett until she was screaming her release creaming Grace's flushed face, when both women had found their release Marcus raked his dull nails down Grace's back. Gripped her hips and let himself go shooting his hot load deep inside Grace's clinching pussy.

When Marcus regained some of his senses he began releasing both women leaving the plugs in their asses, only to reverse their position placing Grace on the table and strapping Bridgett onto the spanking bench, starting the whole routine over again until all three of them were sated and satisfied Marcus then released each woman pulling the plugs from their asses and carrying each one to the bed before he climbed in and fallowed them into sleep.

Conner rose from the cold floor and walked quietly over to the cabinet that held the toys available for the bidders to use opening it with a soft click he glanced behind him to see if it had woken the bitch. Satisfied she was still asleep he looked through the toys till he found a small sharp tool picking it up he shut the door and winced when he heard a stern command.

"Sub what are you doing at over there?" her firm tone did nothing for him but getting caught he had to play his part. So, turning he gave her a plausible answer.

"I was looking for a toy for you to use the next time." He turned with a length of chain in his hands.

The lady rose from the bed walking over to pull out a straight back chair.

"Sit." She commanded

Conner walked over and sat with the chain resting on his lap.

The lady slapped him across the face before picking up the chain to restrain him. With that complete she straddled his lap rubbing her wet pussy against his limp cock.

"You are only allowed to move when I tell you to sub." She said licking the blood off his lips before slapping him again then standing to go to the cabinet herself.

When she returned, she had an electric prob in one hand and a metal switch in the other. Flicking the switch down across his thighs as she came back to him setting the prob on a nipple smiling as his cock twitched between his thighs.

"I don't think you mind well sub." She said as she touched his other nipple with the electric current causing his cock to twitch again before moving around him flicking the switch hard against his shoulder blades.

"And do you know what happens to subs that don't mind?" she asked flicking his back again.

"No what...?" He asked with a nasty sneer in his voice.

The switch came down across his chest several times before the lady came back into his line of sight.

"They get punished." She stated before slapping him again setting the prob on his balls turning it on full, getting a harsh cruse from him in response.

The lady laughed in his face and watched his cock twitch and harden, and when he got close to cumming she fisted it pumping until he creamed her hand, she then took it to his mouth and demanded he clean his seaman off it while she kept the prob on his balls getting him hard again, dropping the prob she straddled him once more incasing his cock in her wet gripping pussy, fucking him until she screamed her release into his mouth as she licked his cum off his lips and tongue, leaving him in a heightened state as she went back to the bed and fell asleep.

As the little bitch slept curled on her side Conner drifted into sleep chained to the chair sliding into the dream.

He was sitting in the pub three weeks after he had taken care of Cora and her fake Master trolling for a new sub. He looked up as he brought his pint up and it slipped from his hand crashing to the floor forgotten as he stared at a dead man.

Conner woke with a start.

Stupid little whore, Conner though as he watched the sun rise out the window. She put a winkle in his plans by waking up when she did, and now he sat chained to a chair with a throbbing cock, and he wasn't even going to get the satisfaction of slitting the bitch's throat. He sat there and stewed as the sun rose higher, then bowed his head when the whore woke again going to shower and prepared to leave, coming out of the shower she fastened the collar back around his throat to lead him back to the Mistress.

In the great hall the next morning the Mistress sat on her throne as the guests brought the subs back, looking at each one thinking that maybe Lilith had gotten used by a guest. But as the last ones filtered in, she was nowhere to be seen. When all were lined up nicely the Mistress rose and gave the closing speech to the guest and then dismissed them to leave the manor and sent the subs back to their chambers.

Conner stood there seething as the Mistress gave her closing speech, just listening to her drone on and on about being thankful and how she hoped they all enjoyed their evening set his teeth on edge, and now he had to wait another month before he could execute his plan.

16

Chapter Sixteen

Marcus sat on the couch and watched as Bridgett paced the room like a caged animal, she looked so angry and confused. He didn't know why it bothered her so much. So, a sub had left it wasn't the first time it had happened, and it more than likely wouldn't be the last. Putting his drink aside he rose and went to her wrapping his arms around her from behind, placing his lips on her throat just below her ear.

"What is it love?" he whispered again her skin.

"What is what?" she asked leaning back against his solid chest.

"Something is obviously bothering you and I want to know what it is." He said biting down with just a little more pain then normal.

When all she did was moan and grip his forearms tight, he let up licking at the bruise starting to form.

"Bridgett."

"I don't know what it is that bothers me so, I know subs have left in the past without a word and I know that there will be others in the future." She pushed at his arms freeing herself and began pacing again.

"I just thought she was starting to come around. She was connecting with Grace and obeying us. I just really thought we were coming to a kind of middle ground with her, and she was starting to find her place." She paced in circles over and over and around.

Marcus once again stopped her in her tracks this time taking both wrists and cuffing them between their bodies.

"You have to stop fretting like this love, you're going to make yourself sick with the worry of it all. A sub left it's as simple as that."

"But she was getting better." She said.

"It doesn't matter now, she's gone."

"But..."

"No." He cut her off forcing her around changing his hands, so he cuffed both hers behind her back with one hand while the other one gripped her hair in a brutal hold.

"Now keep those luscious lips closed and walk." With that he pushed her forward leading her to the back chamber in the room.

"Marcus."

He pulled her head back even more and took her lips in a bruising kiss that left her gasping when he broke away.

"I believe I said keep quite." He stared into her eyes for a long time daring her to say something, when her eyelids lowered in submission, he kissed them softly, and continued walking them into the back chamber.

Once there he walked them over to where he kept the rope, selecting a deep green satin like one he then led her over to a special wooden chair, it had a wide flat seat with high arm rests that had sturdy knobs at the ends, and a high back that looked as if it belonged on a throne with a point in the middle and spindle like spires on each side. Getting her there he turned her to face him and slowly started to bind her wrists in front of her four lopes around each delicate wrist then two to bind them together then he lifted them above her head, hooking them on the middle point of the chair. Taking the excess down her arched back he took each one of the ropes to each thigh wrapping six pretty coils of green satin around her golden thighs then lifting them over the armrests of the chair securing her to hard wood as he pulled her hips forward to rest on the very edge of the seat. Taking just a moment to pet and play with her exposed folds smiling at her wetness.

"Marcus." Bridgett moaned and arched her back even more wanting more touch, more sensation.

Marcus smiled into her clouding eyes and moved his fingers from her wet pussy up to trace her soft lips before slipping them inside for her to suck and lick her flavor off them.

"My pretty little girl, so very confused about everything." He leaned down and licked a bit of her cream from the corner of her mouth before pulling his fingers free.

"You've been dominating to long again love; you know it always makes you think too hard." He gripped her throat and took her mouth in a slow deep kiss sucking and licking the last of her flavor from her lips.

Marcus trailed his wet fingers down Bridgett's throat. Tracing light teasing circles around each nipple, then slid them lightly down the center of her torso teasing at her naval. When she began to quiver and shake, he stopped. Walking away he went to get one of his crops. Returning to her he fallowed the path his fingers took with supple leather, but as he watched her pant in need and desire, he changed his mind on how he wanted to play with her now.

"But I think we need to try something a little different." Saying that he began untying her to left her gently into his arms and carry her to the bed lying beside her he began to stroke her body caressing and teasing her softly worshipping every square inch he touched.

Starting at her face he softly kissed her closed eyes then her nose, he licked lightly at her parted lips before kissing them softly. Moving down he kissed each side of her jaw before stroking one side of her throat while gently kissing and sucking on the other side. Working his way down he rained light kisses across her collarbone moving down to worship at her breasts sucking lightly on one while he gently pinched the other. Keeping his touch ever so soft he moved his mouth over to the other breast and repeated what he had done with the first one smiling at her mewling whimper.

Moving lower he rained soft kisses side to side working his way slowly down her torso, when he reached her hips, he lightly licked at each hipbone before moving down to rain kisses on her shaved mound then gently parted her wet folds to blow cool air across her heated flesh smiling as she gasped and reached out to grip his hair. When he blew air across it again, she moaned gripping his hair tighter trying to pull him closer, but he refused to budge holding her in place as he started to flick at her clit ever so lightly loving her whimpers, moans, and breathless begging. Finally, he leaned in and gave her a long firm lick then sucking hard on her clit getting a cry of ecstasy from her lips.

Now he moved his body slowly back up hers sliding slick skin against slick skin and reaching her mouth he claimed it as he oh so slowly slid his throbbing cock into her wet tight fiery pussy, fucking her deep and slow feeling every quiver, pulse, and spasm of her core. He groaned against her mouth when she gripped his ass tightly, then moaned when she tried to thrust her hips up to meet his. He broke the kiss with a nip to her lower lip.

"Oh no love, I'm still in control, and we're taking this nice and slow." Saying this he repositioned his hips pinning her more firmly to the bed and started his slow teasing slide all over again.

Bridgett gasped and moaned as Marcus started to move again, oh so slowly. Her body kept gripping and closing around his looking for that release into bliss, but he kept her always on that edge making her wait. It had been a while since they had played this way, and she had to say she missed it. The slow drugging feeling of being taken over the edge ever so slowly, and the soft gentle slide of his hands and lips causing her to feel every little thing. When he paused with his throbbing cock fully incased in her tight channel she gasped and gripped his upper back raking her nails down when he set his lips against her throat and bit down hard. Bridgett screamed in bliss as she took that long fall over the edge into bliss, and as her walls clinched and pulsed around his cock, she felt him thrust his hips hard before she felt the hot wet fiery liquid that was his cum shooting deep inside her hot still pulsing core.

When Marcus released his bite at her throat and gently pulled away from her rolling to the side she whimpered, and shivered from the loss of his body heat, but soon he was pulling her into his arms and holding her tightly against him stroking her back as they both came back down. She sighed a soft sound and nuzzled into his side as she drifted off to sleep.

And as Marcus slowly fallowed Bridgett into sleep somewhere down the halls Conner lay awake stewing over his missed opportunity weeks before. The question was why was he waiting? It's not like he really needed to wait for an auction to take place, and it would actually be better without one. Fewer people to take care of, not that he really minded killing more, it would just be easier. So, making up his mind he slipped from his bed and gathering the thing he would need to complete the deed he slipped from his room to carry out his plan.

First, he went down the hall and one by one he crept into each of the little whore's rooms and quietly slit each of their throats as they slept their peaceful sleep, then when he reached Grace's room, he pulled out a cloth and closed it over her mouth and nose smiling when she woke with a start and thrashed slightly before the drugs took effect. When she was out, he carried her into the playroom and binding her wrists suspended her from one of the hooks in the middle of the room, then went off to find the Mistress and her little lap dog so he could finally get what he wanted most.

Creeping into the Mistress's chamber he wandered around and found nothing, so with a frustrated cruse he went off to search the lap dog's room. And well well well what did we have here, he found the two of them in a hidden chamber that was set up as a playroom of its own all cuddled up nice and snug. Walking quietly up to the side of the bed he watched them sleep for a time, then when the Mistress rolled to her back, he made his move swiftly placing the drugged cloths over their mouths and knocking them out before they even knew what had happened. Now going to work Conner carried the Mistress into the playroom displaying her in the same manner two feet from where Grace hung still unconscious and going back for Marcus, he dragged his limp body into the playroom and tied him to a chair facing the two women, so he had a full view of whatever Conner decided to do to them. Finally, he went over and got three ball gags out of a drawer securing each one in turn before using smelling salts to awaken his guests so they could begin.

When Marcus came awake the first thing, he saw was the tariffed eyes of Grace staring at him from where she hung from the ceiling with a ball gag in her mouth similar to the one that was in his mouth and turning his head slightly, he saw the same with Bridgett. What was going on.... The last thing he remembered was falling asleep next to Bridgett in his playroom.

"Don't' try to think too hard, things will be a little fuzzy for a bit." Conner said this as he came into Marcus line of sight from between the two women, stroking both at the hip with the flat side of two deadly looking daggers.

"I think it's about time that you and I had a little talk lapdog." Walking over to Marcus Conner repositioned the daggers in his hands and when he reached Marcus, he thrust the blades into the fleshy part of both Marcus's thighs. Laughing an evil laugh as Marcus screamed around his gag.

"See, you took something of mine a while back, and now I think it's time I take something of yours, and if I burn the house down around you when I'm done do you think you'll stay dead this time?" Conner whispered this in Marcus's ear before pulling the daggers free only to thrust them into his shoulders pinning him up right in the chair.

"Now I want you to watch every little thing I do to your whores, and maybe you might finally understand that you don't take what's not yours." Saying this Conner walked behind the women and picked up a metal barbed flogger.

Conner walked over to the women caressing each of their backs in turn before stepping back and bring the flogger down in a forceful blow across Grace's back causing her to scream from the pain of it, then turning the flogger in hand a few times struck Bridgett's back with a blow twice as hard getting a scream from around her ball gag, and he smiled.

"A little different coming from a sub that really never liked you, isn't it?" he laughed, and rained six more hard blows on each of their backs before dropping the flogger and turning them around so Marcus could see the bloody marks on their lovely back.

"You see lapdog I believe every little whore needs to obey her master in every way. In short lay on her back and take whatever is given to her. And my pretty little whore Cora knew that, until you came along." Conner then back handed Marcus with a force that moved the chair a few inches.

"Now I'm going to play with your disobedient whores while their helpless for me, and all you can do is sit there and watch." Pulling one of the daggers from Marcus's shoulder Conner went to Grace.

Turning her back around he started at her right elbow making small shallow cuts down her side to her hip bone before taking the blade in one long shallow line over to the other side and starting the shallow cuts up to her left elbow enjoying her little whimpers and mewls as he went. He then circled each one of her nipples with the tip watching as they peeked with arousal. He then slid the blade in between the strap of the gag and her cheek leaving his hands free.

"You see they like the pain." He said to no one in particular as he slid his hands down to gripped and play with her breasts, he strokes his thumbs over her piercings smearing them with blood.

"It doesn't matter if it's soft pain or hard pain, it's the pain that gets them off." He stated this then ripped Grace's piercings from her nipples laughing at her screams and the tears leaking from her eyes, then licked at the blood seeping out of the holes left in their place.

He then took her bound hand from the hook and with a hand gripped in her hair forced her over to Marcus making her straddle his legs, he then fucked his hard cock into her pussy and stopped.

"You see the desire in her eyes, don't you?" he asked with an evil laugh as he fucked her slow.

"She'd begged for more if I let her, you should feel her pussy. It's gripping me so tight." He smiled and licked at her throat as he pulled the dagger free of the ball gag and found his release, he slit her throat spraying her blood on to Marcus before tossing her lifeless body to the side.

Marcus watched helplessly as Conner brutalized Grace feeling her body shaking in pain and fear as Conner raped her on his lap, and when Conner slit her throat Marcus raged uncontrollably around his gag thrashing against his bounds as Grace was tossed aside. Then the back hand came again.

"None of that now, you brought this on yourself, and we have one more to go." Conner said pulling the other dagger free of Marcus's shoulder.

When Conner turned Bridgett around there where tear streaming down her cheeks, and as she stared at Grace's crumbled body on the floor Conner stroked her cheek with the blade.

"Now now, she was a good little whore. Take relief in that on your last moment, and we'll see how good you are." He left a thin slice on her cheek the blood mixing with her tears.

Stepping back, he began the same path he took with Grace down the right side with a deep cut across Bridgett's middle before taking the dagger up her right side. This time when he circled Bridgett's nipples with the dagger, he took it so much deep carving each nipple off in turn frowning when she didn't make a sound. So, he carved a deep x into her abdomen then back handed her forcibly when he again didn't get a response. Cursing viciously, he unhooked her arms and practically threw her onto Marcus's lap.

Bridgett's hands landed against Marcus's abdomen, and she stroked him softly with her fingers before Conner gripped her hair and thrust his cock into her ass. When he shifted her slightly to the left, she was able to move her hands to the ropes at Marcus's right wrist and she began loosening them as Conner fucked her, when she felt the dagger at her throat, she closed her eyes so Marcus wouldn't have to see her life leave her body.

Conner threw Bridgett's body on top of Grace's with disgust.

"That bitch of a Mistress doesn't learn.... The whores are supposed to respond. What's up with that, you didn't teach her well enough." Conner sliced the dagger across Marcus's chest.

"That's right, I saw the two of you in your chamber. The Master let's his little whores play. What a joke." He sliced at Marcus's chest again.

Conner continued ranting and slicing at Marcus's chest, but on the eighth blow Marcus was able to get his right hand free and catch the blade before it made contact jerking Conner's wrist around, and the struggle began. Somehow in the fight Marcus was able to slice through the ropes on his left wrist and break free of the chair, but as the two men grappled on the floor a candle was knocked over and the fire started. Not taking the time to think Marcus twisted the dagger and plunged it into Conner's gut, with the last of his strength he went to gather Bridgett and Grace's bodies in his arms and fled the burning manor to the woods.

Marcus staggered around the woods until he found a hidden cave and then entering it, he collapsed. Succumbing to his wounds he died with Bridgett and Grace still in his arms.

17

Chapter Seventeen

When Marcus came back, he lay there taking stock of how his body felt, had it been hours or days since he had carried them all out of the manor. He blinked twice and slowly turned his head at the sound he heard, and he saw Bridgett there holding Grace's lifeless body in her arms rocking gently as she cried. He gingerly rolled to his side and to his knees crawling over to her. He wrapped his arms around the both of them he cried with her for the loss of their precious little pet.

Hours later Marcus and Bridgett walked hand in hand back to the manor, and when they came out into the clearing all they could do was stand there and stare. The manor was down to a few fragments of the stone walls standing.

"Sire, Mistress." Charlie's voice sounded so weak and small they both turned and saw him walking from around the side of the burnt remines of the manor.

"Oh my god Charlie are you okay?" Bridgett left Marcus to go hug their butler and friend and check to see if he was hurt in anyway.

"I'm fine Mistress, since last night was my night off, I wasn't here, but when I returned this morning, I found only the rubble of the manor. What happened?" he returned Bridgett's hug then stepped back to stare at them.

"You're covered in blood."

"We know Charlie, my past came back to haunt me and the whole of the manor paid the price. I'm just glad you didn't get hurt in the process." Marcus came up beside Bridgett and hugged Charlie in turn.

Bridgett sigh and leaned into Marcus, the manor was gone, Grace was dead her blood still dried on the both of them. They now had to find some clothes and bury Grace before the lynch mods came looking for their heads. So, they walked hand in hand with Charlie fallowing behind to the crumbled stone looking for the hidden floorboard that led to the underground office where they had some cloths and their stash of go cash.

While Bridgett got dressed Marcus pulled Charlie aside to talk to him.

"Charlie, the Mistress and I are going to be leaving the country, and I was wondering if you'd like to come with us. You've been working for us for more than fifteen years now, and I'm sure you've noticed that we're not like other people." Marcus said as he pulled on a pair of pants and a shirt.

"Yes, sire I have noticed some things, but it's never been my place to question you or the mistress. I would be honored to continue working for you." He bowed slightly at this.

"Good, it would make things a bit smoother if we had someone, we trusted helping us. So, here's what I'd like you to do. The Mistress and I are going to take some time for just the two of us, but I'd like you to go ahead of us and get a house set up before we arrive." Marcus led Charlie over to where Bridgett was now dressed and getting their papers and cash together.

"Bridgett love, Charlie is going to be coming with us to help take care of things." Marcus rubbed her arms and kissed her temple.

"That sounds good." She said leaning into his touch.

After gathering what they needed they walked with Charlie out to the detached garage.

"Okay Charlie I acquired a small cruise ship a few decades ago that is docked at a marina near Monaco that has been closed up. I would like you to go and start opening it up and airing it out. As well as find a crew and get it setup as a small gambling get away." Saying that he handed

Charlie and envelope that had a passport for Charlie as well as a credit card some cash, and the paperwork for the yacht and marina as he led Charlie to a sensible two door sedan.

"Just leave the car in long term parking and we'll deal with it in time." Marcus shook the man's hand and helped him into the car.

They buried Grace in the woods marking her grave with a stone circle and purple flowers that matched the color of her eyes.

Now as they drove along the coast with their stash of quick cash and some clothes, Marcus picked up Bridgett's hand from where it was resting on the center console kissing her knuckles, he rubbed it softly against his cheek.

"We'll get through this." He said.

"Together." Bridgett said squeezing his fingers.

"Yes, together." He leaned over to kiss her temple.

Several hours later Marcus pulled down the long dirt drive glancing over at Bridgett sleeping in the passenger seat. Slowly easing his way down the narrow road, he turned slightly revealing a log cabin buried in the woods. Parking the car, he got out circling the hood to open Bridgett's door stroking her cheek softly as he undid her seatbelt only to lift her into his arms carrying her to the cabin, and into the single room structure. Making sure to secure the cabin Marcus then removed his clothes before slowly stripping Bridgett of hers. It was time to take some time for just the two of them, starting here in their little hidden heaven in the woods.

Two days later Marcus was on his back in bed with Bridgett straddling his waist rubbing her clit against his hard stiff cock, he groaned sliding his hand up her thighs to grip her hips pulling her down to grind hard against her sensitive folds. Loving the sensations as she placed her hands on his chest raking her fingernails down leaving red welts and a trail of glorious pain in their wake.

"That's right love, make it hurt." He demanded grinding harder.

"Yes, now, more." Bridgett panted rubbing harder before repositioning to thrust his cock into her tight hot core.

Digging her nails into his chest deeper she threw her head back moaning loudly as she started rocking a slow torturous rhythm. Marcus dug his fingers into her hips urging her on silently. He smiled up at her when she slid her hands up to circle his throat leaning in to kiss his lips fucking him hard as she squeezed his throat.

"Oh, so good, Master loves it when I play." She sucked his lower lip between her teeth biting hard smiling as his hips jerked against hers.

"that's right love, Master loves it, give me more." He begged when she released his lips

Bridgett smiled a soft smile.

"More Master says." She released his throat, raising her hips, and slipping his cock free.

Nipping at his lips once more she crawled up his body, turning around to straddle his face placing her dripping pussy at his mouth.

"Eat me Master please." Bridgett begged.

she leaned down to begin licking her juices off his stiff cock slowly before sucking it deep into her throat swallowing over and over groaning around him as he licked, nipped, and sucked slurping up her juices. Bridgett stroked his thighs up and down ending at the junction where his hips mt his thighs sliding up to grip, squeeze and teases his balls delighting as he hardened in her mouth. Sucking harder as he groaned against her clit flicking and sucking it before working his mouth down to fuck his tongue into her entrance.

Reaching up Marcus palmed her ass rubbing before spreading her cheeks licking up to tongue her puckered asshole flicking and teasing it as she groaned around him sucking harder as he dug his fingers into her fleshy ass causing some of the pain she loved. As he made his way back down to her entrance to fuck it with his tongue her began bobbing her head faster and faster panting around him as he brought her closer and closer to the edge. When she screamed around him soaking his face with her juice, he thrust deeper into her mouth causing her to gag slightly and suck harder and harder until he groaned against her shooting his hot cum deep down her throat. Releasing him and gasping for air Bridgett stretched herself out pulling her hypersensitive pussy away from his mouth she kissed his ankle lightly stroking his calf softly as she drifted down from her high. He smiled smugly stroking her calf as he drifted down, and they both fell into sleep.

Over the next two-month Marcus and Bridgett stayed locked inside the cabin consumed with each other, loving but never over dominating. They loved and healed.

18

Epilogue
    Six years later

Marcus stood on the balcony overlooking the blue waters of the Mediterranean sea a drink in his hand, with a hot tub on the deck of the ship off to his right. Turning his head now he looked across the deck to where Bridgett lay naked stretched out asleep on a chase lounge set up in the shade, one arm draped across her toned middle. Her golden skin an even darker dusky shade looking more bronze than gold, he loved running his hands over its heated flesh watching her eyes go wide and haze over with desire as he kneaded her breasts before pinching and tweaking her peeked nipples or worked his finger slowly through her slippery wet folds that pulsed and gripped at him begging for more. He sipped at his drink continuing to stare at Bridgett when he heard the subtle clearing of a throat behind him.

"Are they here?" he asked without turning.

"Yes, sire they are, shall I wake the Mistress?" Charlie asked from behind him.

"No, I'd like to speak with them first. Thank you." He heard Charlie walk away as he finished his drink staring at his sleeping beauty.

Leaving the empty glass on the railing he turned and headed back into the cabin suite. Entering through the glass doors he could see the young couple standing in the foray due to the open concept of the grand suite, the entryway living room dining room and sitting room of sorts all flowing together to form one large room with little walls and slight curves to give some separation. Walking around the furniture Marcus surveyed the couple. The woman was more than a foot shorter than the man with dark hair and tanned skin, she had a slight almond shape to her brown eyes and a little bow of a mouth. Her tits were large and on display in a low-cut form hugging top, and her hips flared nicely inside her tight jeans. The man was about Marcus's height with paler skin and golden hair that was cut close to his head, his eyes were sharp and smoky blue staring back at Marcus as he approached.

"Hello, I'm Marcus one of the owners of the ship you are on, Welcome to my suite." He held out his hand as he reached them shaking each of their hands in turn.

"Hi, is there a reason you've asked us here. Is there something wrong with our ship board account." The man said shortly.

"No, no, nothing like that. I'm sorry if I've alarmed you." Marcus rubbed the back of his neck sighing.

"No, I've been keeping an eye on the two of you yes and doing some asking around. But the reason I've asked you here is to see if you two would be interested in playing with another couple?" He asked staring into the man's eyes.

The man paused seeming to contemplate the question, then he turned looking into the woman's eyes. When she nodded slightly, he smiled bending in for a kiss. The man broke the kiss holding his hand out again.

"Yes, we'd love to play, I'm Dan, and this is my wife, Lana." He shook Marcus's hand.

"Fallow me, I'd like to show you something." Marcus turned and led them through the sitting room, opening a door that led to the suite next door.

"Welcome to our playroom." Marcus said flipping a switch revealing an almost thousand square foot space of BDSM toys.

"Wander around and make yourselves at home, now I have to go and tell my lovely Bridgett the plan." He smiled ruefully.

Marcus walked back into the main suite wondering if Bridgett would even go for this plan he had concocted, it had been just him and her for the past six years, and he was getting concerned. Not that he didn't enjoy their play it was just that they had never gone this long without bringing others into their play in a long time. Stopping at the cabinet of liquor in the sitting room to pour himself a fresh drink before heading back out to the deck to wake Bridgett.

Heather Ross is a budding new author that lives in Washington state. She enjoys reading, and crafting when she is not writing, along with doing ren fair like events, and camping with family and friends.